GABBy
DuRan

Triple
Trouble

ELISE ALLEN & DARYLE CONNERS

LOS ANGELES · NEW YORK

ALSO BY ELISE ALLEN & DARYLE CONNERS
GABBY DURAN and the Unsittables
GABBY DURAN: Troll Control
GABBY DURAN: Multiple Mayhem

Text copyright © 2019 by Elise Allen & Daryle Conners

All rights reserved. Published by Disney • Hyperion, an imprint of Buena Vista Books, Inc. No part of this book may be reproduced or transmitted in any form or by any means, electronic or mechanical, including photocopying, recording, or by any information storage and retrieval system, without written permission from the publisher. For information address Disney • Hyperion, 77 West 66th Street, New York, New York 10023.

First Hardcover Edition, November 2019
First Paperback Edition, May 2021
10 9 8 7 6 5 4 3 2 1
FAC-025438-21085
Printed in the United States of America

This book is set in Adobe Caslon Pro, Little Boy Blue, Taberna Script, The Hand/Fontspring; Officina Serif ITC Pro/Monotype
Designed by Marci Senders

Library of Congress Control Number for Hardcover Edition: 2019017183
ISBN 978-1-368-05442-3
Visit www.DisneyBooks.com

SUSTAINABLE
FORESTRY
INITIATIVE

Certified Sourcing

www.sfiprogram.org
SFI-01054

The SFI label applies to the text stock

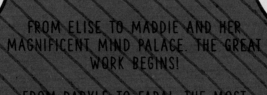

FROM ELISE TO MADDIE AND HER
MAGNIFICENT MIND PALACE. THE GREAT
WORK BEGINS!

FROM DARYLE TO FARAI, THE MOST
ENCOURAGING FRIEND, WHO HELPED
LAUNCH GABBY INTO THE UNIVERSE!

FOURTH DOSSIER

Triple Trouble

The following chronicle details an incident so highly restricted, it has merited an entirely new classification level:

Supremely Sensitive Secret Hush Hush

a.k.a.

SSSHH

Only those members of the Worldwide International Government with clearance level Ultrillion-Cubed may even glance at the contents herein. Any leak would not only break the bonds of the Asset Recharacterization Program, but also risk lives in all corners of the Greater Galactic Cooperative.

With such dire consequences at stake, even those with the proper clearance should think twice before delving in. Should you feel you'll have the burning inclination to reveal even the slightest hint of what you're about to read, it is absolutely imperative:

DO NOT TURN THE PAGE.

WELCOME BACK, TRUSTED FRIEND, TO THE
FOURTH AND POSSIBLY FINAL DOSSIER OF
ASSOCIATE 4118-25125A, A.K.A. GABBY DURAN,
SITTER TO THE UNSITTABLES.

chapter ONE

"**b**ob, wait!"

Gabby Duran wiped the curls out of her face and ran even faster. Her sneakers pounded on the ground, and her purple knapsack bounced against her back as she raced across the massive lawn to catch up with her charge.

"BOB!"

Bob was nine years old, and he loved to run wild. Gabby had been babysitting him regularly for about six months, so she knew this about him, and had a million different ways to keep him settled and occupied. Yet sometimes none of them worked, and he'd bolt for the thick hedge surrounding his family's property.

"Bob, come back! We'll play tag! You're it!"

That usually did the trick. Bob loved tag. But this time he didn't turn around and start chasing her. Instead he leaped up and dove through the closely packed branches.

Gabby grimaced. Without breaking stride, she yanked a pair of gloves out of her jacket pocket, pulled them on, covered her face with her hands, and crashed through the bushes right after him. She felt the branches scrape over her body, but she'd dressed in jeans, her purple puffer jacket, and thick socks for just this reason, so it wasn't a problem at all. It technically wasn't even a problem that Bob had left his property, since the hedgerow abutted a public park with wide fields and a playground—the perfect place for a kid to run free.

What *was* a problem was that Bob was bright green, about half the size of a fire hydrant, and shaped like a comma, with a big, round bulb of a head and a long, thin, spring-curled tail. He had no discernible eyes, nose, or ears; a giant mouth splayed across his top like a headband; and as he bounced through the park on his coiled tail his voice rang out with a slight metallic clang, "BOI-OI-OI-OI-OING! BOI-OI-OI-OI-OING! BOI-OI-OI-OI-OING!"

2

Bob was an alien.

Specifically, he was a Boingle, from a planet in the Sproidelly Nebula. Gabby knew this not from Edwina, her boss at the Association Linking Intergalactics and Earthlings as Neighbors (A.L.I.E.N.), but from Bob's parents, who always liked to chat as they were getting ready for a night out. Not that Gabby could understand their language—to her it sounded like the humming warble of a tuning fork. But the tones somehow communicated directly with her cell phone, leaving texts that Gabby could read, though A.L.I.E.N. always erased them mere moments after they arrived.

The park was crowded, and people were starting to notice the bouncing alien child. A girl in spiral curls who looked around eleven and her equally curly-haired younger brother looked up from their family picnic and stared, while a teenaged boy got bonked in the head by a Frisbee because he was so distracted. Even the dogs in the park took notice: a golden retriever and a wiry white terrier stopped chasing each other and raced in wide circles around Bob as he blithely bounced along.

This should have stopped Gabby's heart. When Gabby started babysitting for A.L.I.E.N. almost a year ago, Edwina told her the one, vitally important rule: never let humans see aliens. Now here was Bob, bouncing in full view of a whole field of staring people, but Gabby wasn't worried at all. The second she'd emerged from the hedges, she'd shrugged off her purple knapsack, yanked out a large remote control, then swung the bag back over her shoulder. Now she poured on speed, pressing buttons and adjusting the joystick while she chased after Bob.

"Daddy, look!" the picnicking curly-haired boy cried out. "That girl's got a bouncing RC toy!"

"Sweet," the Frisbee guy called as Gabby ran past. "Where'd you get that?"

"Dunno!" Gabby called back. "It was a gift. Online, I think."

It was always a good answer. People knew you could find anything online. They also liked easy explanations. As long as Gabby had a reasonable excuse for the faceless bouncing creature, people would accept it.

At least, most people would. Even as she tried to act natural, the skin on Gabby's neck prickled, and she kept her eyes peeled for anyone who looked suspicious—anyone who might be from G.E.T.O.U.T., or another organization eager to expose the aliens living secretly on Earth. If any of them saw Bob and tried to grab him . . .

"Gabby!"

Gabby looked up and saw a girl her own age racing

toward her—a twelve-year-old with long, blonde hair so smooth and shiny, it billowed behind her like a silk curtain.

Madison Murray. What was she even doing here? This park was miles away from their neighborhood.

Gabby plastered on a smile. "Hi, Madison! I'm kinda doing something right—"

But Madison spread her arms wide and slammed Gabby into a hug that sent them both sprawling to the ground. The remote control popped out of Gabby's hands and rolled away.

"I got it!" called the curly-haired boy. He looked about five years old, and Gabby didn't even realize he'd been following her on his stubby little legs until he scooped up the remote and started pressing its buttons.

Gabby's heart thudded. Kids were smart. It wouldn't take him long before he realized the remote did nothing. Then Bob wouldn't be a toy; he'd be a living creature Gabby couldn't explain away.

With a mighty groan, she rolled out from under Madison, then leaped to her feet and snatched away the remote. Her heart hurt when the little boy's face fell and his lip puckered out, but she had no other option.

"Sorry!" she cried, already running after Bob again. "My parents gave it to me. I promised no one else would touch it!"

"BOOOOOOOOING!" Bob bounced ten feet in the air, leaping over an elderly couple on a park bench. Gabby quickly slammed a remote button and hooted out loud, as if the feat had come from her.

The little alien was near the far edge of the park now, close to a copse of tall trees. Beyond those was a busy street. If he bounced out there . . .

"I can't believe you made a little boy cry, Gabby."

Madison Murray had gotten back to her feet and was already matching her step for step. While Gabby was breathless and sweaty, Madison practically floated by her side. When she smiled, she lit up like the sun, and her words were filled with just as much warmth. "You must have had a really good reason. So where are we running, bestie?"

Gabby shook her head, hard. It had been ten months since A.L.I.E.N. had to erase parts of Madison's memory, but Gabby still wasn't used to the changes in her one-time-mortal-enemy's personality. They'd lived across the street from each other their whole lives and both were dedicated to music—Madison to the flute and Gabby to her French horn—but picture-perfect Madison had always looked down on her rumpled and klutzy neighbor and did everything in her power to bring Gabby down. It only got worse when Gabby started babysitting for aliens. It was like

Madison could smell the secret, and she and her cell phone always showed up at the wrong time to try to bring it to light.

Then Gabby accidentally brought Madison onto an alien spaceship.

The memory wipe that came afterward was only supposed to affect those specific memories. It succeeded in that and didn't *really* seem to touch anything else ... except the way Madison felt about Gabby. Madison came out of the wipe with no memory of their antagonistic past. Now she adored Gabby to the point of hero worship. She had even traded in her frilly dresses for jeans with purple T-shirts and high-tops.

Honestly, Gabby liked nasty Madison better.

"BOI-OI-OI-OI-OING!"

Gabby had finally caught up with Bob and was only two steps behind him when he leaped to the highest branch of a tree. Craning her neck, Gabby saw his blank head turn left, then right, searching hopelessly for a way back down. She heard him start to whimper.

"I've gotta get him," she said out loud, then tossed down her knapsack and tore it open.

"Him?" asked Madison.

"*It,*" Gabby corrected herself. "The toy. I got it stuck."

She yanked two flat, oblong pieces of metal from her

knapsack. Each one had thick straps on it and fit perfectly over Gabby's shoes. She grabbed the ends of the straps to pull them tightly, then shrugged her knapsack on again. "Be right back," she said to Madison.

Gabby kicked her heels together. The metal flats hummed to life, then powerful springs shot out of the bottoms and zoomed Gabby straight into the air. She wobbled and pinwheeled her arms to stay upright.

Zee, Gabby's actual best friend, had made her the shoes. From the second she'd found out the details of Gabby's new job she'd wanted to be involved, but since Gabby couldn't actually let her help with the babysitting—except in emergencies, of course—Zee had settled for being Q to Gabby's James Bond, outfitting Gabby with a zillion different gadgets she might need in case of alien emergency. The spring shoes had come in handiest, but Gabby still felt like she was one small lean away from breaking every bone in her body whenever she used them.

She bounced off the ground once . . . twice . . . three times, always keeping her eyes on Bob, until she finally reached his height.

"Don't worry, Bob," she said to the frightened alien. "I've got you."

She reached out and wrapped her arms around the little

guy's coiled body, pulling him off the branch. As they sank back to the ground and bounced to a stop, he cuddled his head against Gabby's chest.

"Great save, Gabby!" Madison cheered, waving her cell phone in its crystal-studded pink case. "I got the whole thing on video!"

"You what?!" Gabby was so shaken up she forgot she was holding an alien.

"Uh-huh." Madison smiled proudly. "I already posted it to InstaChat!" Then she frowned. "Your toy is squirming. Is there a problem with the batteries?"

"No. It's fine." Keeping Bob tightly in her grip, Gabby kicked off her shoe covers, grabbed them with one hand, then walked quickly back across the park. "I'm sorry—I gotta go. Babysitting job."

"I'll come, too!" Madison chirped. "I'm waiting for my mom, but she's shopping. She won't be back for a while. I bet the kids you're sitting would love to meet your best friend!"

"You'd think so, right?" Gabby said, walking even faster. Bob was still wriggling, and if she didn't get him home soon, she'd lose him again. "But this family's pretty serious about their privacy. And I know you wouldn't want to get me in trouble, right?"

Madison's eyes widened as she gasped out loud.

"Never!" she said. She stopped in her tracks and called after Gabby as the distance grew between them. "See you soon, BFF! Miss you till then!"

Two seconds later, Gabby felt her phone vibrate in her pocket. She was almost positive it was a text from Madison. Something with a lot of heart and smiley-face emojis.

Gabby ignored it. Instead she whisked Bob back through the hedges and onto his own property, where she set him down on the grass. He coiled up, ready to bolt away again, but this time Gabby was prepared.

"You *could* go . . . but then you'd miss these."

She plopped down cross-legged on the lawn, unzipped her knapsack, and burped open a reusable container. The strong scent of fresh-baked bread wafted through the air, and Bob boinged right up to Gabby, gently nudging her with the front of his head, urging her to hurry up. Gabby laughed. She couldn't explain it, but she had yet to meet an alien who didn't go nuts for breadsticks from her friend Satchel's family pizzeria. Once Gabby discovered that, Satchel made it his business to bring her a daily batch.

"Catch!" Gabby called, and she broke off a piece of breadstick and tossed it across the lawn. Bob bounced through the grass to get it. Then, since his mouth splayed over the top of his head, he somersaulted over the breadstick to chomp it down. Gabby giggled and drew back her arm to throw another piece.

It was that image that froze on a giant screen as Gabby Duran, A.L.I.E.N. Associate 4118-25125A, stood on trial for crimes against the Worldwide International Government and the Greater Galactic Cooperative.

chapter
TWO

"Stood" on trial was a bit of a misnomer, of course. Gabby was actually sprawled out in a large, plush recliner with a massage function that was probably meant to be relaxing, but instead just felt like someone was rolling a carburetor up and down her spine. The chair was tilted all the way back, giving Gabby a clear view of the planetarium screen above, which was still filled with her own smiling face.

"For the love of Zinqual," a familiarly sharp voice rang out from somewhere to her left. Edwina sounded like she was right next to Gabby, but even though Gabby turned and squinted through the darkness, she couldn't see anything at all. "I fail to see how Gabby feeding the child has any relevance at all. If anything, it strengthens her case that she's an excellent babysitter."

Gabby grinned. Despite the situation, it felt good to hear Edwina say something nice about her. Most of her compliments were backhanded at best.

"You really think I'm an excellent babysitter?" Gabby asked.

She could see nothing, but she swore she heard Edwina's eyes roll. "Yes," the woman said drily, "but you're a terrible defendant. Now wipe that smile off your face; it's wholly inappropriate.

"As for you," Edwina continued, raising her voice to talk to others in the room—Gabby thought of it as a room, though she hadn't walked in a door and had no idea if there were any walls or even a floor—"if this footage is all you have, it's both immaterial and remarkably unflattering. Honestly, do you even own a hairbrush, Gabby?"

"There are some things of material relevance in the clip," a meek male voice interjected from somewhere near what Gabby imagined to be the ceiling. "Like the breadsticks. I was wondering, Ms. Duran, do you have any on you?"

"Any breadsticks?" Gabby asked, confused. "Um . . . probably . . . I always have some in my knapsack. . . ."

Gabby leaned over one side of the recliner, then the

other, and felt around for her knapsack, but it wasn't any-where. Alarmed, she felt around more frantically. "That's weird. I don't see it. I never go anywhere without my knap-sack." Then she froze, feeling dizzy as a chill washed over her. "I don't even remember coming here," she admitted. "How did I get here?"

"You're not here, obviously," Edwina's voice said. "You're asleep in your room. It's the electrical impulses from your brain that we've harnessed to bring your consciousness to this trial."

Gabby squirmed in her seat as the rolling oil drum inside the recliner pressed against her rear end. It certainly *felt* like she was here. "Are you sure I'm still in bed?"

Edwina didn't answer, but Gabby could easily imagine the white-haired woman glaring at her, one eyebrow raised. Yet when Edwina spoke, it wasn't directed to Gabby at all.

"Even if she had the breadsticks," Edwina called out to the voice up above, "they would only be a figment of her mind and impossible for you to eat. So if that's all—"

"No that's not all!" boomed a different male voice, this one loud and imperious. "We also have *this*!"

The image on the planetarium screen changed. Now it showed an open laptop computer, its screen filled with an article from something called *The Third Eye*. Below the screaming headline "GABBY DURAN: FLYING GIRL!" was a picture of Gabby from when she'd bounced up to retrieve Bob from the tree. It had been snapped from below, and from that angle it did indeed look like she was flying. Gabby recognized the shot immediately and she rushed to explain.

"That's the picture Madison took. She posted it on InstaChat and tagged me. That's how the *Third Eye* people know my name. They messaged me, and I told them the truth—I'm just bouncing on the shoes Zee made. I even put them in touch with Zee and she told them all about it. She was excited to! She—"

"There is an *alien* in that picture," a woman's voice said icily.

"Where?" Edwina asked. "Can you point to the Boingle? Can you see even the slightest outline of him?"

Gabby leaned forward in her seat, and not just because the recliner's massaging roller was now boring into her skull. She squinted, but even though she knew exactly where Bob was in the shot, and even though the picture itself was blown up to the size of a massive billboard, she couldn't see him at all.

"You cannot," Edwina finished, "in part because of the angle of the shot, and in part because his skin blends in perfectly with the tree's leaves. This is nothing but a ridiculous tabloid article, and it never once even hints at an alien child's presence."

"It doesn't have to!" The loud man's voice was shrill now. "It labels Associate 4118-25125A as a *Flying Girl*! You know what kind of girls fly on Earth? Alien girls, or girls with access to alien technology. And it's no help calling this a 'ridiculous tabloid.' You know as well as I do that our enemies monitor tabloids, and if they suspect Associate 4118-25125A is working with us, or worse—is an alien herself—she can't possibly do her job. The life of every alien child in her care will be in jeopardy. And, not that it matters, but *her* life will be in jeopardy!"

"Not that it matters?" Gabby echoed.

"Gabby's life is in jeopardy all the time," Edwina said. "That's immaterial."

"Wait—*all the time*?" Gabby asked.

"It's hardly the first mistake Associate 4118-25125A has made," the icy female voice noted. "Need we remind you of this spectacle?"

The picture on the giant screen switched to an image of a cafeteria in chaos. Food trays flew in every direction, and students and teachers gaped in shock as a two-foot tall, hot-pink fuzzy hat swung on a hanging light fixture.

The hat was actually an alien named Wutt—Gabby's very first babysitting job from A.L.I.E.N.

"It looks bad," Gabby admitted, "but Wutt was fine. No one knew she was an alien. She even—"

"Or this?" the woman asked, and the screen switched again, this time to a troll child standing horizontally like a flagpole on the side of a building, leering down at Gabby's friend Satchel, who stood pale and open-mouthed, and looked like he was about to pass out.

"Okay," Gabby said, "but you have to understand—"

"Or *this*," the woman continued. And the image changed again, this time to the suburban cul-de-sac where Gabby, Satchel, Madison, and Zee had landed with the Tridecalleon babies when they'd zapped off a spaceship and back down to Earth. The entire cul-de-sac was roped off with caution tape, several black vans sat at the entrance, and Gabby saw Edwina holding out a small bunny to Madison—the bunny that would erase all her memories of alien activity.

"The blonde girl wasn't the only one whose memory we had to adjust that day," the woman said. "We were only lucky that more people weren't at home. And these are only the beginning."

The giant screen began to strobe now, image after image flickering by, one immediately after the other. There was

Gabby in science class, her eyebrows still smoking from an encounter with a fire-breathing Dragornian; there were Satchel and Zee clinging to Gabby's legs as she soared away on a six-year-old Blimperwill she'd tried to pass off as a parade balloon; there was the crowd of people at the beach pointing and staring at Gabby's astounding "surfing" skills when she had actually just leaped on to a Mermoid girl to stop her from swimming away.

There were so many images that by the time Gabby recognized one, twelve more had flipped past, but the idea was clear: an endless parade of Gabby's Greatest Mistakes. When the screen froze back on the *Third Eye* article, the loud man's voice returned.

"And now *this*," he railed, "which is the final straw and leaves us no choice but to shut down the Unsittables program for good!"

Everything went silent. Gabby didn't dare breathe. Was this really it? Was A.L.I.E.N. actually firing her?

"I'm afraid I have to agree," said a new voice. This one was also female but younger, and it seemed to resonate from all over. "My ruling is that the Unsittables program is—"

"Wait, Your Honor," Edwina said. "I will be the first to admit that Gabby Duran is far from an ideal Associate. She has shown herself to be careless, overly trusting, and often takes risks that are nothing less than absurdly shortsighted."

"Um, Edwina? Maybe I should be representing myself. Your Honor—"

Gabby tried to sit up, but the massage chair changed to squeeze mode—its sides squished around her so tightly she could barely breathe.

"She also cares deeply for alien children," Edwina continued, "and every single mishap in that poorly edited montage—"

"Hey, I went to film school!" interjected the meek-voiced man.

"—was a direct result of Gabby going out of her way to try to accommodate these children, and make them happy while keeping them safe. You will also note that despite every lapse of professionalism, none of these children have been harmed or exposed."

"We've been lucky," replied the icy-toned woman.

"No," Edwina said. "We've been in good hands. Which is more than I can say for Gabby herself, who appears to be turning blue. Can we get rid of the chair?"

"I thought it would make her more comfortable," the meek-voiced man said, but an instant later the chair was gone, and Gabby was instead floating in the complete darkness. Her body tilted backward, so she was stuck upside down, her knees tucked in and her arms floating out at her sides, like she was submerged in deep water.

"The chair actually was more comfortable," she said as she struggled to right herself. "Do you think maybe you could—"

"Besides," Edwina said, continuing her thought, "we can't make any decisions right now. The P.T.A. meeting is tomorrow. The fate of the entire universe rests on Blinzarra, and she can't attend without a proper babysitter."

The meek man, the blowhard, and the icy woman all started talking at once, but the voice of the judge sliced through them all.

"Enough! Edwina is correct. Our Unsittables program is still new and has exactly one sitter: Associate 4118-25125A. We need her."

"You do?" Gabby's body had started uncontrollably rolling in midair. If she hadn't been so nauseous, she would have felt proud. "I'm really the only one?"

"We'll see how she does," the judge continued, ignoring Gabby's question, "and we'll judge her competency afterward. That is all."

Gabby heard the *BOOM!* of a gavel pounding on wood, over and over. *BOOM! BOOM! BOOM!*

Then Edwina's voice whispered right in her ear. "It's settled. The future of the Unsittables program rests on you successfully babysitting during tomorrow's P.T.A. meeting. I suggest you don't screw it up."

"Wait, what P.T.A. meeting? I'm not scheduled to work tomorrow. I'm supposed to help my mom at the fair. Edwina?"

BOOM! BOOM! BOOM!

The booming wouldn't stop. It kept going and going until Gabby bolted upright in her own bed, and it turned into the equally loud *BOOM* of a boxing glove, ferociously pounding the side of her bed.

chapter
THREE

gabby rolled over the pile of laundry rumpled up with her comforter and leaned off the bed to smack a big red button on top of a heavy metal cube, which was Zee's latest attempt to make Gabby a successful alarm clock. The cube held a timer and a boxing glove, and when it was time to get up, the glove shot out like a cuckoo and slammed into Gabby's bed until she woke up.

Gabby's phone dinged with a text, and she dove back under the covers to find it. The text was from Zee.

Got an alert ur alarm went off. Did it work?

Gabby wrote back: *Yes. And thx. You saved me from bizarro dreams.*

Gabby tossed her phone back on the bed and trod over more dirty clothes. She flung open her door and zipped to the bathroom, but it was already occupied by her little sister. Carmen sat cross-legged on the bath rug in the middle of the room. She was fully dressed in plain brown pants, soft with no tag; an equally soft and tagless shirt with no collar or buttons of any kind; and slip-on moccasins. Her hair hung perfectly straight, with the bangs cut as she preferred them: in a precise horizontal line across the very top of her forehead. Carmen was the most organized member of the family, so she kept track of their household finances, as well as all the appointments for Gabby's babysitting and Alice's catering business. One of those big leather ledgers sat open in Carmen's lap; the others were splayed on the floor around her.

"Car?" Gabby said. "How come you're sitting on the bathroom floor?"

"Someone's downstairs with Mom," she said dully, never taking her eyes off the ledger in her lap. "And I'm already dressed, so I can't go back to my room."

Carmen had very specific ideas about things. Gabby pushed back about them sometimes—it was her job as big sister to periodically give Carmen a hard time—but only when she thought Carmen could take it. Right now her sister looked too put out to handle anything more. Gabby didn't even ask her to move. She just stepped around her while she did what she needed to do.

"Who's with Mom?" Gabby asked as she reached for her toothbrush.

"Someone peppy," Carmen said with as much disdain as she could muster in her voice. "Dad called earlier. You missed him."

"Carmen! Why didn't you wake me up?"

Not waking Gabby for a call from Dad was as close to familial treason as Carmen could get. Their father, Steven Bruce Duran, had served in the army, and for most of Gabby's life had been missing in action and presumed dead. Gabby hadn't wanted to believe it. For a while she even thought maybe her dad had been involved with A.L.I.E.N., too, since Gabby had randomly received his dog tags from an alien she once babysat. Yet even though she held out hope that somewhere in the universe he might still be alive, her heart had always known he was gone.

That's why she was gobsmacked when he rang their doorbell on Carmen's birthday.

He'd shown up right when she was opening her presents. Gabby was so little when he left that she wasn't even sure it was him; Carmen hadn't even been born at the time, so she didn't recognize him at all. To her he was just some stranger infiltrating the very specific present-opening ritual she insisted on following every year. But when their mom burst into tears and wrapped her arms around him, Gabby understood that her greatest wish had come true. She ran over and threw her arms around them both, and in that moment she knew they'd be a family again, and this time nothing would tear them apart.

She wasn't right about that. Not exactly. Her dad had been away a long time, and both he and Alice had changed a lot over the years. Plus Alice had a boyfriend—the dreaded Silver Fox—but to Gabby's delight Alice dumped him so she and Gabby's dad could give it a real shot.

It didn't work out. They tried, and they both swore they still loved each other . . . just not in the same way. They might have been each other's soulmates once, but now they weren't a match. So when Dad got a job opportunity in Miami, he took it with Alice's full understanding and support. And when Mom got back together with the Silver Fox, Dad was just as supportive . . . even if Gabby wasn't.

The whole thing was a roller coaster when it happened, but in the end it was good. Alice and Steven weren't like those divorced parents on TV who hated each other; they ended things really well. And Steven wasn't one of those dads who disappeared on his kids. The day he moved, he gave his word that he'd be involved in Gabby's and Carmen's lives. He said they'd see each other as much as they could, and to make sure they stayed close in between visits, he asked them to promise to tell him everything that happened in their lives. Gabby agreed, but she knew she was lying. She wasn't allowed to tell him one of the biggest things in her life—that she babysat for aliens on Earth.

She wished she could, though. Especially since there were all kinds of things he couldn't remember about the time he was away. He knew he'd been captured, he knew he'd been rescued, he knew there was time he spent under-cover when he couldn't contact them ... but some of the details were fuzzy, in the same way Madison would have been fuzzy about the details around the time she went into space. Gabby's dad also didn't react to his dog tags the way Gabby thought he might. When she showed them to him, she'd said she couldn't remember where she'd gotten them. He just shrugged and said he must have lost them overseas and the army must have sent them back. It definitely didn't seem like he was trying to hide some alien connection, but maybe there was one he had forgotten.

Zee agreed—she for sure thought Steven's disappear-ance had something to do with aliens. Satchel took the other side; he thought Gabby was just automatically seeing aliens everywhere. Edwina wouldn't give her any information whatsoever; she encouraged Gabby to just be happy her father was back in her life.

She *was* happy he was back. Really happy. Which is why Carmen not waking Gabby to tell her he was on the phone was such a cardinal sin.

"Carmen!" Gabby said—or tried to say around the toothbrush she now had in her mouth. "I asked you—why didn't you wake me up?"

"Not my job. I'm not an alarm clock," Carmen said.

Gabby rolled her eyes. She held her toothbrush in her teeth and tilted back her head so the spit wouldn't drip out of her mouth, then pulled out her phone and held it up so she could text her dad. *Sorry I missed your call!!!!! C didn't wake me!* 😭

He texted back almost immediately. *Because she's not an alarm clock?* 😄

Gabby smiled as best she could without dribbling. She loved that he already understood. *Zactly. Call u later?*

Yes, he replied. *Love you.*

"I hope you didn't say you'd call him later, because you're busy," Carmen said. "You have a job today."

"No I don't," Gabby said as she went back to brushing. "I'm taking the day off to help Mom at the fair, remember?"

"I remember that's what you *said*," Carmen replied, her eyes and pen still on the family's budget ledger. "But you told this client that you'd babysit so she could go to a P.T.A. meeting."

Gabby frowned as she filled her bathroom cup with water and started to rinse. A P.T.A. meeting . . . That sounded familiar. . . .

Then she did a spit take, hitting the mirror instead of the sink, and splattering toothpaste-water everywhere.

"Disgusting," Carmen said, again without raising her eyes.

Gabby held the edge of the sink and took deep breaths. A P.T.A. meeting. That's what Edwina had said in Gabby's dream—that she'd be babysitting so someone important—Blinzarra?—could go to a P.T.A. meeting.

She'd also said the future of the Unsittables program depended on how Gabby did.

"What's the client's name?" Gabby asked.

Carmen looked up at her and raised an eyebrow. Gabby sighed and rolled her eyes, then grabbed a towel and wiped up the mess she'd made. "Better?"

"Still streaky," Carmen said. "There's Windex and paper towels downstairs in the kitchen under the—"

"Carmen!"

Gabby lunged for the giant tome with all her appointments in it, but Carmen slapped her hand on top of the book.

"Mine," she said firmly.

Gabby acquiesced and took her hand away. She tried not to smile as Carmen opened the book, because of course that's exactly what Gabby had wanted her to do. Sometimes Carmen was amazingly easy to play.

"'Ms. Jackson,'" Carmen read. "Says 'Gabby promised she'd babysit during P.T.A. meeting.'"

Gabby thought it over. "Jackson" didn't sound much like "Blinzarra," but if it was an A.L.I.E.N. appointment, Edwina would have changed the name to something that sounded human and not at all suspicious.

"I'll text you the address," Carmen continued. "The appointment's at eleven thirty, and it's approximately forty minutes away on your bike, assuming you ride at a moderate speed."

"Eleven thirty?" Gabby pulled her phone back out and looked at the screen. "It's ten o'clock now. You should have woken me up!"

Carmen opened her mouth, but Gabby cut her off before she could say it. "You're not an alarm clock. I know. Move over. I need space."

Carmen didn't budge, so Gabby went ahead and washed up as quickly as she could, torqueing her body every which way so she wouldn't step on her sister or get her ledgers wet. Then she ran back to her room and sniffed clothes from the floor pile to sort the waiting-to-be-put-aways from the waiting-to-get-tossed-in-the-washes and pulled on the first clean clothes she found. Throwing her purple knapsack over her shoulder, she ran downstairs and into the kitchen to grab some breakfast . . . and slammed into a tripod with a camera mounted on top of it. The tripod tipped, but a large, bearded man lunged and saved it.

Gabby, on the other hand, smacked into the floor.

"Gabby!" cried her mom. "You're just in time! We're going to be on TV!"

Gabby got to her feet and looked toward the sound of the voice . . . but what she saw didn't look like her mother at all. Alice Duran was the definition of low maintenance. She always wore her hair naturally curly, let it stick up in Einstein-like spikes, barely put on makeup, and dressed for pure comfort in yoga pants and oversized shirts. When she was cooking for her catering company, she usually wore an apron so loved and used, it was covered with ancient stains that wouldn't come out even after several washes.

Today, however, Alice's hair was long and silky, flowing in gentle waves down to just below her shoulders. She wore form-fitting jeans that tapered at the ankle, with fashionably ripped patches on the knees. Her blouse—it was definitely a "blouse"—was turquoise and fitted: a short-sleeved button-down with the top few buttons open in a way that was tasteful but clearly meant to be attractive. Even her face looked different. She wore red lipstick that brought out her ultra-white teeth, her eyes were perfectly lined and shadowed, and . . .

"Did you pluck your eyebrows?" Gabby asked, incredulous.

Alice held up a finger, smiling at the rotund cameraman and a remarkably coiffed-and-made-up redheaded woman sitting at their kitchen table. Then she took Gabby gently by the arm and led her aside.

"Isn't this exciting?" she whispered. "Dina Parker from the local news is doing a piece on me! Well, all of us, really—all the local chefs coming together to make the world's largest pizza at the fair."

"Wow," Gabby said. "I didn't know giant pizza would make the news."

"Not the *news*-news. Dina does all those kooky special feature stories. She's so good on camera. Just look at her."

Gabby followed Alice's gaze. Dina was still sitting at their table, but now she held up a mirror and adjusted her already-flawless makeup.

Was Gabby imagining it, or had Dina angled her mirror in just the right way to watch Alice and Gabby as they spoke?

"Did I ever tell you I used to dream about being a TV journalist?"

That grabbed Gabby's attention. "No! Seriously?"

Alice nodded. "When I was a kid. Long before I went to school for chemistry and ages before I even dreamed I'd end up a caterer, I wanted to be on camera, just like her. Bigger though—like, you'd see my face on the side of buses and billboards—and mugs! And I'd be on commercials." She turned away from Gabby, then whipped her head back around, as if posing for the camera. "Alice Duran, evening news."

Gabby laughed. "You'd have been great!"

"Well, sure," she said playfully, "I'm great at everything I do. Just like my kids. But with the catering I got to stay home for you and Carmen. You never know, though—maybe this'll be my big break. I'll be so good on camera, I'll get discovered and *I'll* be the next Dina."

She winked at Gabby, then practically floated back to the reporter. "Okay, Dina, I'm ready!"

"Wonderful!" Dina said. She rose to her feet, then looked at Gabby. Her eyes widened in surprise as if she were noticing her for the first time, but there was something fake about it. Gabby was now positive Dina had been checking her out in the mirror.

"You must be Alice's famous daughter! Gabby Duran, right? Babysitter to the Unsittables?"

If Gabby still had toothpaste-rinse in her mouth, she'd have done another spit take. As it was, her throat simply closed up.

"Unsittables" was code for the aliens she babysat. No one was supposed to know about them. No one but A.L.I.E.N. . . . and their enemies.

chapter
FOUR

"excuse me?" Gabby croaked out.

"Oh, please," Dina said with a conspiratorial smile. "I know all about how you babysit for Adam Dent and Sierra Bonita. Everyone else says their triplets are terrors—totally unsittable. But I hear they're little angels for their favorite babysitter."

Gabby hadn't realized she'd stopped breathing until she started again. Adam Dent and Sierra Bonita were big movie stars, and it was true that Gabby was their favorite sitter. They'd flown her to movie sets all over the world to babysit for Ila, Lia, and Ali. Their secrets were just as important to Gabby as A.L.I.E.N.'s, but at least information about them wouldn't threaten the fate of the galaxy.

At least, she didn't think so.

"I don't discuss people I babysit, Ms. Parker," she said. "But I don't think it's very nice to call little kids 'terrors.' They're just kids."

Dina somehow managed to keep her smile painted on, even as her lip curled in a brief sneer. "Of course. I'm sure they're lovely. But we don't have to talk about them. Maybe you'd rather talk about being a flying girl?"

The reporter snatched her tablet off the kitchen table and showed Gabby what was on the screen: the same *Third Eye* article that had been splayed across the planetarium in her dream.

If it *was* a dream. Gabby had major doubts that it was. She was also starting to majorly doubt that Dina was actually here for Alice, even though she'd never say that out loud. Alice would be too disappointed.

"I don't fly," Gabby explained. "The story's wrong. My friend Zee made these springs I put on my shoes and—"

"Fascinating, yes," Dina said, clicking off the tablet, "and I suppose that is more reasonable, but my spidey-sense tells me that you still have all kinds of fascinating secrets, even if flying isn't one of them."

35

Dina crossed her arms across her red suit jacket and raised a perfectly plucked eyebrow. Gabby had the uncomfortable sensation the reporter was looking inside her mind.

Then Alice placed her arms on Gabby's shoulders and leaned in close. "*I* have fascinating secrets!" she said. "Like the secret ingredient for the biggest pizza crust in the world!"

Dina grimaced, but by the time her eyes met Alice's she'd transformed into her usual beaming self.

"Wonderful!" she said. "I can't wait to hear all about it. And I'm sure Gabby and I will have lots of time to talk when I'm watching you and the other chefs work your magic at the fair. Right, Gabby?"

"Actually, I can't go to the fair," she admitted, far more to Alice than to Dina. "I have to babysit."

Both Dina and Alice said, "Really?" at the exact same time, but only Alice looked upset. Dina looked like a vampire who smelled blood.

"You promised me you'd come watch," Alice said, and not even her perfect layer of cosmetics could hide her disappointment.

Gabby's heart broke a little. Alice did everything for her and Carmen, and she didn't ask for a lot in return. For a second Gabby considered canceling on her client, but the truth was she couldn't even if she wanted to. She had no way to get in touch with "Ms. Jackson." Whatever number A.L.I.E.N. had left for Carmen would only go to Edwina, and she'd never let Gabby ditch. And while it seemed unlikely that some P.T.A. meeting would affect the future of the universe . . . Gabby had seen stranger things.

"I know. I'm really sorry. I promise I'll try to get to the fair in time for the official measuring. It's just that there's a big P.T.—" She stopped herself, just in case Dina knew more than Gabby did. "There's an emergency."

"An emergency!" Dina gushed. "This is so exciting. Charlie, roll film."

"That's a great idea," Gabby said, maneuvering Alice in front of the camera lens. "You can get all the world record pizza rules on camera. Like, it's not just about the size of the pizza, right, Mom? You have to have enough toppings on it, too?"

"You remembered!" Alice flipped her hair like a pro and beamed at the camera lens. "That's absolutely right, ladies and gentlemen. There's a lot that goes in to making the world's largest pizza, and I'll be happy to tell you exactly what it takes."

Gabby caught Dina trying to glare at her as she slipped out of the room, but Gabby just waggled her fingers, grabbed her purple puffer jacket, ran out the front door . . . and screamed as she nearly ran into Madison.

"Bestie!" Madison cried, and threw her arms around Gabby's neck for a huge hug. When she pulled away, Gabby noticed Madison looked like her old self again. She wore a pink fuzzy sweater over leggings with a black-and-white checkered pattern. Her blonde hair hung long and smooth, and she'd gone beyond her normal pink lip gloss to add what looked like eyeliner and shadow.

She looked beautiful, Gabby supposed, but weirdly overdone for a Saturday morning.

"Hi, Madison," Gabby said. "I'm kind of in a hurry. . . ." She tried to edge by and get to her bike, but Madison stepped in front of her.

"I got you a present," she blurted. She thrust out her hand, which held something small and rectangular. Gabby knit her brows. Presents out of nowhere was a change. Maybe the mind-zapping was affecting her in new and different ways. She'd have to mention it to Edwina.

"Thanks, Madison."

"Open it!" Madison said, bouncing giddily as Gabby took the rectangle. Gabby hadn't realized it hinged, but she now opened it to reveal a swath of shiny pink with a tiny brush on one side and a mirror on the other.

"Lip gloss?" Gabby asked.

"Same shade as mine!" Madison said. "We can be lip-twinsies!"

Gabby noticed the divots in the gloss and the pink color on the brush. "*Is* it yours? It looks used."

Madison's cheeks flushed, but her smile remained wide. "Well, yeah! That's what makes it meaningful—I'm giving up something of mine, just for you."

"Okay," Gabby said warily.

Madison was *definitely* acting weirder than usual. Gabby didn't even wear makeup, not regularly. Even if she did, it would never be cotton-candy pink lip gloss—never mind *used* cotton-candy pink lip gloss. Still, it seemed easier not to ask too many questions. She slipped the lip gloss deep into her jacket pocket. "Thanks," she said.

"My pleasure!" Madison said. Then she craned her neck to try to see around Gabby. "Um . . . I noticed the news van in front of your house. Was that Dina Parker I saw walking in?"

Madison smoothed her hair and rubbed her glossed lips together, and Gabby instantly understood. The "present" didn't have anything to do with the mind wipe or their new bestie status at all. Madison just wanted to be on TV.

"It was," Gabby said. "She's interviewing my mom about the world's largest pizza. She's pretty into weird and unusual things, so you never know—if there's anything weird and unusual you can show her, she might want to interview you, too."

Madison's eyes widened and her mouth dropped open. Gabby knew exactly why and she tried not to laugh. "Weird" and "unusual" were two words Madison would never want associated with her, but now they were exactly the qualities she needed to get on TV? Her brain was totally short-circuiting.

Then Madison gasped and put her hands to her cheeks. "I was named most popular girl in school every year—even when I was in Baby Buckaroo! That *has* to be a record! I'll go get the ribbons." She broke into a run back to her house across the street. "Thank you, bestie! LoveYaMeanIt!"

Gabby grinned as she made her way to her bike. Sometimes it was fun having the new Madison around. It definitely cost her time, though. She needed to hurry if she wanted to get to her job on time.

Putting all thoughts of Madison, news reporters, and giant pizzas out of her mind, Gabby quickly snapped her phone into the holder she'd installed on her bike handlebars, punched in the address Carmen had given her, then strapped on her helmet and rode off at top speed, wondering what A.L.I.E.N. had in store for her this time.

chapter
FIVE

"Edwina tells me you're a pro, so it should all be very easy," Blinzarra said as she sat on a bench in her foyer and pulled on a pair of thick-heeled leather boots. "Sharli's in the living room, watching TV. If it were up to her, she'd sit there all day, so if you could pull her away for a little while, that'd be great."

"If it's okay, I'll keep the TV off," Gabby said. "I like playing with the kids I babysit. It's more fun."

Blinzarra stopped mid-zipper and looked at Gabby, amazed. "Bless you," she said. "You're a better woman than I."

She bent back over her boots and continued her monologue as she moved her belongings from one purse to another, swung on her long coat and cinched the belt, then gathered her keys. Gabby listened, but she almost didn't have to—it was the same spiel she'd heard a million times from a million different parents. Honestly, it was so normal that Gabby wondered if Blinzarra was even an alien. Maybe she was just a human being who worked for A.L.I.E.N. Gabby had found that most aliens—even the ones who looked completely human—had *something* that gave them away, at least when they were with Gabby and didn't need to pretend. Maybe their head spun all the way around, or they lapsed into a native tongue that sounded like a teakettle's whistle, or they sprouted an extra arm to gather their things. Blinzarra did none of that. She looked like a regular mom, her hair in long, natural curls, tamed by a vibrant headband. She wore a professional-looking belted dress, boots, and the jacket, and never did or said a single thing that didn't strike Gabby as one hundred percent Earthling.

"We recycle our bodily wastes internally, so you don't have to worry about the bathroom," Blinzarra said. "Though we do have one for you if necessary."

Okay, *almost* one hundred percent Earthling.

"I hate to say I'll be out of reach," Blinzarra went on as she gathered the last of her things and stood by the door, "but I really will. If there's an emergency, Edwina will get a hold of me. She said you know how to reach her right away?"

Gabby didn't; not exactly. After all this time she still didn't have a cell phone number or email for her boss. But Gabby usually found that if she really needed her, Edwina somehow knew. So she didn't feel like she was lying when she said, "Absolutely."

"Great. Right in here." She took a step down the hall, then stopped short and smacked her palm into her forehead. "Oh. I hope you don't mind. My friend Lester dropped his son, Petey, here, too. Ten years old, really good kid. Lester's wife, Mayvrell, was supposed to be home to watch him, but she had a family thing come up. I would have asked in advance, but it all happened at the last second, and Lester's on the P.T.A. organizing committee, which means he had to get there early—"

Blinzarra was speaking a mile a minute. Gabby could tell she felt bad about the situation, so she jumped in as soon as she could to put the woman's mind at ease. "It's okay," Gabby said. "I understand. Things happen."

Blinzarra let out a huge sigh and smiled. "Edwina was right. You are amazing. And don't worry, we'll double your fee for the extra child. Come on."

Gabby grinned—Edwina had called her amazing! That was two compliments in less than twenty-four hours!—and followed Blinzarra as she clomped down the hall and into the kitchen, then made a left to enter a carpeted family room with three plush sofas and a recliner. Eschewing all of them, a three-year-old girl with a head full of braids instead sat cross-legged on the floor in front of the TV. A brown-and-white springer spaniel lay next to her, with its head in her lap.

"Awww! You have a dog!"

The dog didn't get up, but its tail thumped at the sound of Gabby's voice.

This was new. The only pets Gabby had ever seen in alien homes were aliens themselves, and they never wasted time acting like animals in front of Gabby.

"We do. Sneakers is a good boy." Blinzarra walked over to them and kissed both Sharli's and Sneakers's heads, then she remained crouched close to Sharli. "I'm leaving, okay? Be good and do what Gabby says."

"Okay."

Sharli didn't take her eyes off the TV as Blinzarra gave her one more kiss before she stood to go.

"Love you!" Blinzarra called.

"Mwah!" Sharli called back. The three-year-old kissed her palm, then raised her hand high and opened and closed it, as if sending the kiss to her mother. Blinzarra made a show of catching it, even though Sharli wasn't looking. "Got it. Thank you, baby!"

Blinzarra gave Gabby a final good-bye, then walked down the hall toward the door.

"Wait!" Gabby said. "Where's Petey?"

"He's around," Blinzarra said. "He likes to hide sometimes, but he doesn't go far and he'd never leave the house. Thank you again!"

Blinzarra walked out the front door. While Sharli kept her eyes on the TV, Gabby wandered around the kitchen, looking for all the places a ten-year-old might hide. The pantry door was ajar and Gabby smiled.

"Petey?"

She pulled the door open, positive she'd see a grinning boy crouched inside . . . but it was empty. So was the back hall and the space between the washer and dryer. Gabby returned to the family room. She peeked in all the spaces between the three couches and behind the recliner, and even pulled back the floor-to-ceiling draperies that framed the sliding glass door to the backyard, but there was no sign of Petey.

He really did like to hide.

That was okay, though; Gabby knew some kids needed time to come out of their shells. She'd give him his space and eventually he'd emerge and say hi. In the meantime, she plopped down on the floor next to Sharli and her dog.

"Mind if I pet Sneakers?"

Sharli shook her head, but she didn't look at Gabby and she didn't say anything. She just pointed at the TV.

"You like this show, huh?" Gabby said. "Okay. I promise I won't interrupt. But once it's over, we'll turn it off and do something else that's just as fun."

Gabby petted the dog as she watched the show, paying close attention to the story. It wasn't always easy to get a kid to turn off the TV, but if Gabby came up with a game based on a show they loved, that made it simpler. It helped that Gabby knew this show, and it wasn't hard to get the gist of the storyline. She kept her mouth shut throughout the episode—she'd promised not to interrupt, and her number one rule for babysitting was *Always keep a promise*—then grabbed the remote and turned off the TV.

"Okay!" Gabby said, hopping to her feet. "So we're gonna play the show. You're the pink puppy, I'm the green puppy, Sneakers is the yellow puppy, and this couch is our headquarters, so we'll hop up and get our mission—"

But when Gabby threw herself onto the couch . . . the couch howled.

"OWWWWW!"

Gabby jumped like her body was on fire. "What was that?!"

Sharli didn't answer. She just narrowed her eyes and looked at the couch . . . at which point one of the seat cushions rose three feet and floated in thin air. Gabby was so mesmerized by the floating cushion, she didn't even notice the far stranger thing the cushion had revealed.

"Ooooh . . . you're gonna be in trou-ble," a voice singsonged.

Gabby looked down at the now-cushionless couch . . . and saw a tiny male figure, about as tall as a box of crayons. He looked around ten years old, and wore jeans, a gray-and-black T-shirt, and little running shoes. When Gabby knelt down for a closer look, she saw his shoes were scuffed, his jeans were grass-stained, and his short brown hair had a small cowlick that stuck straight up on top of his head.

"Petey?" Gabby asked.

The boy, who had to be Petey, didn't look at Gabby; he craned around her to look at Sharli, hands on his hips, swinging them back and forth as he taunted her. "You moved stuff without as-kin'. . . . I'm gonna tell your mo-om . . . and you're gonna get it ba-ad. . . ."

FOOMF!

The cushion dropped back down on top of him.

"Hey!" Gabby cried as she quickly yanked the pillow back off the couch. "We don't crush our tiny friends with pillows."

Unlike *Always keep a promise*, this wasn't one of Gabby's go-to rules, but it felt like a good one.

Luckily, Petey seemed fine—more angry than hurt. He stood back up, put his hands on his hips, and narrowed his eyes at Gabby. "I'm not 'tiny.' I'm exactly the right size for a ten-and-three-quarters-years-old Minisculean."

Gabby felt bad that she'd insulted the boy. "Right," she said quickly. "I apologize. You're not tiny at all. Petey, right? I'm Gabby."

Petey didn't answer; instead he rose into the air. For a second he looked down, surprised, then he kicked and flailed his arms. "Hey, cut it out! Sharli, come on!"

Gabby wheeled around and saw the little girl staring intensely at the boy, a hint of a grin on her lips.

Gabby knew better than to get angry. That would only egg Sharli on.

"Sharli, I'm going to count to three, and I expect you to put him down. One . . . two . . . thr—"

Sharli glanced away from the boy. He screamed as he plummeted. Sneakers barked and ran over as if to help, but

Gabby held out her cupped hands and caught Petey. He folded his arms and grimaced. "I hate when she does that."

Gabby held him up to her eyes to get a better look. .

"Cut it out," Petey said. "It's not nice to stare. And if you keep holding me this close to your face, I'll tell you about the hair I see growing on your nose."

Gabby blushed and thrust her arms out. "Sorry. I wasn't staring. I mean—I didn't mean to . . . Really? A hair on my nose?"

She shook her head. Now wasn't the time to think about that.

"Let me start over. I'm Gabby. I'm babysitting while your parents are out, and I think you, and Sharli, and Sneakers, and me should all have fun and play a game together."

"Hold on a sec," Petey said. He ran across Gabby's arm, leaped off and grabbed the hem of her T-shirt, then swung back and forth on it until he had enough momentum to let go and soar down to the coffee table. He held out one finger—one more second—then leaned his whole body into pushing a stack of books across the table to a tall glass of water. He trotted up the book spines like stairs, pulled a tiny straw out of his jeans pocket, dunked it in the water, took a sip . . . and did a spit take, spraying water everywhere.

"You want me to play with *them*?!" Petey snorted.

"BO-RING! Sneakers won't run when I try to ride him, and Sharli's a *girl*. She likes dolls and stuffed animals and she barely even talks. She's—"

Petey's body suddenly zipped into the air, turned upside down, then dunked into the glass of water, again and again and again.

"Hey!" he spluttered between dunks. "Cut it out! That's *not cool*!"

"Sharli!" Gabby snapped.

Petey thumped down on the coffee table as Sharli turned away from him and looked at Gabby. Her bottom lip poked out and her big brown eyes filled with tears.

"Oh no . . . oh no . . ." Gabby scooted to Sharli and wrapped the little girl in a big hug just as she started to sob. Gabby felt awful. She had never snapped at a kid she was babysitting and made her cry. *Never*. "I'm so sorry, Sharli. It's just—you could have really hurt him."

It flashed through Gabby's mind that Petey was an alien, so even though he looked human, things didn't necessarily work the same way. Maybe he *could* breathe with his entire head underwater. Maybe he had gills, or breathed through his kneecaps, and she'd just made a three-year-old cry for no reason.

Out of nowhere, a vivid image filled Gabby's head. Petey, standing on the back of the couch, making faces at

Sharli. He waggled his hips, stuck out his tongue, and held his hands like moose antlers on the sides of his face while he wiggled his fingers.

She didn't *actually* see it; she was still holding Sharli. All she could really see was the empty far side of the room. But the image was so clear, Petey could have been right in front of her.

Then she heard him shout.

"Hey! Come on! Cut it out! STOP!"

For a second she thought she was imagining that, too, but then Sneakers started barking and pawing at her. Gabby let go of Sharli and realized the little girl had been staring around Gabby's back at Petey . . . who was now tumbling quickly backward through the air, screaming all the way.

chapter SIX

"Sharli, please put him down!"

This time Sharli didn't listen. Eyes locked on Petey, she toddled out of the room, sending him spinning backward down the hallway and into the foyer. Gabby gave chase, but Sneakers was ahead of her. His nails scratched the tile floor as he zigged and zagged to keep up with the boy, barking constantly.

"Sneakers, it's okay," Gabby said, but she was honestly just as worried as the dog. Petey was now twirling through the air, coming painfully close to walls and the floor. Gabby leaped and lunged for him, but she missed him every time.

"Keep away from the babysitter!" Petey crowed. He had sounded frightened before, but now that Gabby was chasing him, he laughed like it was a game. "Keep going, Sharli!"

Gabby heard Sharli giggle behind her, then she rocketed Petey up into the air, so fast he was a blur.

He was about to smash into the ceiling.

"Stop!" Gabby cried frantically.

He stopped exactly a nanosecond before his head would have splattered into a pulp. Gabby couldn't breathe. Petey didn't seem worried.

"What's the matter?" he laughed. "Nervous much?"

Gabby sat on the floor and tried to stop the room from spinning. That only made Petey laugh harder. "It's not like she's gonna hurt me."

"Sharli's *three*," Gabby said. "She could hurt you by accident—badly."

"Aw, come on. You wanted us to have fun together, right?" Petey asked. "Help me out, Sharli."

His body slowly descended until he floated right in front of Gabby's face. *Don't reach for him*, Gabby told herself. *It'll only encourage them.*

Then Sharli shook Petey up and down like a can of soda ready to explode. His teeth rattled, and whatever was in his pockets jangled.

"Uh-oh . . ." he moaned, his voice vibrating. His face

looked green, and he put a hand over his stomach. "I don't feel so good ..."

Gabby broke. She reached out to snatch him, but he somersaulted over her head at the very last second. Both kids laughed out loud.

Gabby bit her lips so Sharli and Petey wouldn't see her smile. If torturing Gabby made them happy, well, she'd done sillier things to get kids to play together. And if Sharli kept Petey just out of Gabby's reach, she wouldn't slam him into anything dangerous.

Gabby roared as if she were truly furious and jumped to her feet, lunging and spinning and leaping after Petey, who always zipped away before she could grab him. Sharli went from giggling to shrieking squeals, and Petey laughed so hard he cried.

"Enough!" Gabby finally wailed. She collapsed in an exhausted, panting heap. Sharli squealed and threw herself gleefully on Gabby's head. Gabby laughed ... until she heard Petey scream and realized that without Sharli's gaze on him, he was plummeting to the floor. Gabby tried to pull Sharli off her so she could roll over and catch Petey, but the little girl struggled and Gabby panicked—she knew she'd be too late.

Suddenly, a perfectly clear image filled her mind, just like before. This time she saw Petey land on the soft fur of Sneakers's belly. She even heard the quiet thump as he landed. By the time she peeled Sharli off her and sat up, Sneakers was getting up, and Petey had crawled onto the dog's back. He urged the dog to go faster instead of plodding across the floor.

Gabby shook off the weird sensation in her head. She hadn't been looking at Petey at all when he fell. She was blocked by Sharli, so she couldn't see any of it. It *felt* like she'd seen it, but clearly she'd just heard the thump of Petey landing and imagined the rest.

Except she saw him fall *before* she heard the thump.

And what about earlier, when Gabby saw Petey teasing Sharli, even though her back was to him? Did Gabby just imagine that, too?

"Petey—" she began, but then her phone rang. She pulled it out of her pocket and saw it was Zee. Gabby answered.

"Hey! Can't talk. Babysitting. Everything okay?"

Through the phone Gabby heard a roar of clangs, dings, and whooshes, plus the murmur of a zillion different voices.

"I'm at the fair!" Zee shouted so loudly that Gabby had to hold the phone away from her ear, and both kids and the dog turned to listen. "Satchel's here, too—his aunt and uncle are helping with the world's largest pizza! When are you coming?"

"NOW!" Petey shouted. He slid down Sneakers's back

and ran across the floor so he could shout into the phone. "We'll meet you there!"

"Gabs?" Zee asked. "Who was that? Was that a kid?" Then she gasped. "Was that an *alien* kid?!"

Gabby shook her head in disbelief. "Zee? Tell me you didn't just scream that out loud in the middle of a crowded fair."

There was a long, silent beat, then Zee's voice got even louder. "...in the *movie we saw last night*?! 'Cause that's totally what I'm talking about—the alien kid in the movie we saw last night! Was that who it was ... in that movie?!"

"Nice save," Gabby said, deadpan. "Very smooth."

"Hold up," Zee said.

Gabby wanted to get off the phone, but she wouldn't hang up without saying good-bye, and all she heard on the other end was muffled noise, like Zee was taking the phone somewhere. She put her phone on speaker, then gathered Sharli under one arm and beckoned for Petey and Sneakers to follow them back to the living room. Gabby had already plopped Sharli down on the rug, put the phone on the coffee table, and dug through a toy chest to find some oversized plastic blocks to occupy the girl while Gabby made a fort out of couch cushions, when Zee finally spoke up again. Gabby didn't know where she was, but the outside noise was muted, while Zee's voice was an intense near-whisper.

"Okay, we can speak freely," Zee said. "Who are the specimens?"

"Specimens?" Petey repeated. He sat next to the phone at the edge of the coffee table and kicked his feet off the side. "Is she for real?"

"Kids, Zee," Gabby called over her shoulder as she worked on the fort. "They're kids."

"Well, bring 'em! The fair is great for kids!"

"Yes!" Petey shouted. "Smart girl," he added to Gabby. "I like her a lot."

"I can't," Gabby called to Zee. "I don't have permission from their parents."

"Our parents would *totally* let you take us to the fair!" Petey said. "Call and ask. They'll say yes. Right after they say you destroyed the universe 'cause you interrupted their super-important meeting that'll decide the fate of everything."

"What?!" Zee's voice shot back. "Did he say 'destroyed the universe'?"

"Yup," Petey replied. "One interruption at the wrong time, and kabloooie-uney!"

It didn't really seem plausible that a P.T.A. meeting could decide the fate of the universe, but everyone in her dream-that-wasn't-a-dream last night had made it sound awfully important, so . . .

"Long story," Gabby said into the phone. "Sorry, Zee. I really wanted to be there with you and Satchel—"

"So come! We'll see you soon. The kids, too—and this time I want hair clippings!"

"No hair clippings. *Never* hair clippings."

But Zee had already clicked off.

Petey turned to Sharli. "Didja hear that?"

"Don't worry," Gabby assured him. "She's not getting hair—"

"We're going to the fair!" Petey shouted. He threw both arms in the air and sang. "We're goin' to the fa-ir, we're goin' to the fa-ir!"

"You're not going to the fair," Gabby said. "It's a bad idea."

"It's a great idea!" Petey said. Then he chanted, pumping his fist, "Fair! Fair! Fair!"

"Feh! Feh! Feh!" Sharli joined in, bouncing up and down on her chubby toddler legs. Even Sneakers got caught up in the excitement; he barked along in perfect rhythm.

Of course Petey and Sharli wanted to go to the fair. Gabby did, too. It ran for three weeks every year, but everyone knew the first Saturday was always the best. There were rides, and farm animals, and exotic foods like last year's fried ice-cream hamburger. Almost everyone Gabby knew was there right now, including Satchel and Zee, which was perfect. Satchel was terrific with kids, and Zee would go nuts over a tiny boy and a girl who could move things with her mind. Sure, Gabby would have to deal with Zee's never-ending quest for alien tissue samples, but she'd handled it before and she could handle it again.

Still, there's no way she could bring the kids. "I'm sorry. I can't take you to the fair," she said. "Even if I had permission, it's too far to walk, and I can't get you there on my bike."

"*Duh*—sure you can," Petey said. "I can fit in your pocket."

"That's not safe," Gabby said. "And it doesn't help Sharli. My bike doesn't have a baby seat."

Sneakers whined. He drilled his snout into Gabby's back.

"Ow! Sneakers . . ."

Gabby stood to stop the snout-probing, then Sneakers moved in front of her, grabbed the bottom of her jeans in his mouth and tugged, whining more.

"You okay, Sneakers? You need to go out?"

Sneakers moved back behind Gabby and pushed his head into her knees.

"Looks like he wants to show you something," Petey said.

"Is it your leash?" Gabby asked the spaniel. "You wanna show me where it is so I can take you out?"

Sneakers trotted ahead of Gabby, then turned back, waiting for her to follow.

"Go ahead," Petey said. "I'll watch Sharli."

Gabby gave him a look.

"What, you think I'm too small?"

"No!" Gabby insisted. "It's just . . ." Gabby tried to come up with an excuse that had nothing to do with Petey's size, but she couldn't.

Petey just watched her and nodded, his hands on his hips. "Uh-huh. Thought so. Look." He walked to the recliner, jumped onto the hem of a sweater hanging over the chair back, and shimmied into its pocket. He ducked all the way down. "If she can't see me, she can't move me. I'll peek up to make sure she's okay. See? Small but *smart*."

Gabby blushed. She still wasn't sure it was the best idea to leave the two of them alone, but Sharli was now fully engrossed with the oversized blocks and the room looked very toddler friendly. As long as Gabby only left the room for a little bit and didn't go far, everything should be fine. "If she gets up, yell for me," she said. "I'm just gonna get his leash. Go ahead, Sneakers."

Sneakers led Gabby through the kitchen, down the short hallway, then scratched at a door until Gabby opened it to reveal a remarkably neat garage with a single car inside. Sneakers ignored the car and trotted right to a bicycle with a toddler seat on the back. A child-sized helmet rested on the seat. The dog reared back on his hind legs and put his paws on either side of the helmet, then turned to Gabby, tongue out, as if to say, *See?*

"Oh," Gabby said, surprised. "You're not showing me your leash at all. You're showing me there's a bike with a baby seat."

Gabby furrowed her brow and looked at Sneakers. She and Carmen had never had a dog. She knew a lot of them understood key words and phrases, but it seemed like an awful lot to pick up on "baby seat," then remember it through Gabby's whole conversation with Petey. Unless maybe taking Sharli on the bike was part of his normal schedule.

"I *could* borrow the bike and take Sharli," Gabby said as if the dog could understand, "but there's still no way to keep Petey safe. Plus, I don't have permission."

Sneakers barked, then moved to the front of the bike and nosed a saddle bag that was firmly attached to the frame, just below the handlebars. Sneakers barked and nosed, barked and nosed, until Gabby joined him at the bag.

"Uh-huh," she said. "A bag. I see it."

Sneakers pawed at the zipper.

"O-kay," Gabby said. She pulled open the zipper.

Inside the bag sat a small leather car seat. It mounted securely to the bike frame through the back of the pouch and had a seat belt that would hold its occupant safely in place. Leaning down closer, Gabby saw that the front of the pouch was mesh, making it easy for anyone inside to breathe and enjoy the scenery.

"This looks like it was made for Petey," she said. "You understood that, too?"

Sneakers barked and wagged his tail.

"Okay," Gabby said guardedly. "But what about you? Would I just leave you here?"

Sneakers trotted back into the house, tail wagging, then turned and barked. When she didn't move, he barked three more times in quick succession, like he was impatient with Gabby for taking so long to listen. Fascinated, Gabby followed. She pulled the door closed behind her and trailed him back to the living room, where Sharli was now crawling across the rug on all fours, Petey riding on her back.

"Hi-yo, Sharli! Away!" Petey cried.

Sharli giggled and blew through her lips. As long as she was having fun, Gabby wouldn't stop them.

Sneakers barked again and Gabby turned back to him. He was standing by a dog bed, and once he had Gabby's attention, he pulled a blanket off the bed to reveal a leash clipped to a very dapper green-and-white plaid vest with pockets. Gabby knelt down and took the ensemble in her hands.

"Your leash and jacket. So I can take you to the fair."

Gabby narrowed her eyes and looked at Sneakers. "You understand every word I'm saying, don't you? Are you sure you're a dog?"

Sneakers licked Gabby's face, then he pulled up his two back legs and scooted his butt across the rug.

He was clearly a dog. A super-intelligent alien dog maybe, but definitely a dog.

Sharli crawled up to Gabby, head-butting her in the side. Petey was still on her back. "So can we go to the fair?" he asked. "Pleeeeease?"

"Peeeeeez?" Sharli joined in.

Sneakers reared all the way back on his hind legs and waved his forepaws up and down. He was begging, too.

Of course Gabby couldn't say yes. Sure, she and the kids all wanted to go. The dog wanted to go. They even had the means to go. But *Don't leave home without the parents' permission* was the most basic babysitting rule of all. There was absolutely no way Gabby could break it.

Suddenly, Gabby's cell phone—which was still on the coffee table—rang out with Mozart's Horn Concerto no. 4 in E Flat. It was one of Gabby's favorite concertos since it featured her own instrument, the French horn. It was *not*, however, one of her ringtones, so Gabby simply stared at it, perplexed, as the music played on and on and—

"For the love of Zinqual, Gabby, just pick up your phone!"

The voice was Edwina's. Gabby lunged and grabbed her phone. The music cut off immediately, and text scrolled across a black screen.

Communicating in text so as
not to alarm the child.
She is in severe and imminent danger.
Do not let on, but get out of the
house immediately. All will be well, just
vacate the premises, act naturally,
and await further instructions.

Gabby had barely finished reading when the text disappeared and was replaced by a single word:

NOW

Gabby's heart raced triple-speed, and she heard the blood rush through her ears. When that final word disappeared from the screen, she pocketed her phone and smiled at the kids and Sneakers.

"Okay, you win," she said. "Let's go to the fair!"

chapter
SEVEN

Gabby's head was a steamy marsh under her helmet, and the curls that slipped out hung limply in her face. She hadn't let Petey, Sharli, or even Sneakers see her anxiety as she'd put on their helmets and gotten them strapped and—in Sneakers's case—leashed-and-vested up for their ride. She'd even joked and smiled, though she couldn't remember anything she'd said. Honestly, she was shocked she hadn't just recited Edwina's note, since it was emblazoned across her vision, standing in tall fiery letters:

She is in severe and imminent danger. . . . Get out of the house immediately. . . .

She. That meant Edwina didn't know Blinzarra and Petey's parents had added an extra alien into the equation. That didn't matter though—whether Edwina knew about it or not, Sneakers, Petey, and Sharli were *all* her responsibility. She pedaled fast, standing in her seat to sink her whole body into each stroke. The end of Sneakers's leash was wrapped around Gabby's wrist, and the dog trotted alongside the bike. He seemed happy to keep up with her pace, which was good because Gabby didn't dare slow down.

She is in severe and imminent danger. . . . Get out of the house immediately. . . .

Why? Who was after Sharli? Was it G.E.T.O.U.T.? Had Blinzarra been somehow discovered, and were G.E.T.O.U.T. agents storming the house for her and her daughter? And what would happen when they showed up and no one was home?

Would they keep looking?

Would they come to the fair?

Gabby didn't think so. If A.L.I.E.N. knew someone dangerous was heading to the house, they'd go and stop them. Sharli and Petey would be fine, as long as Gabby got them far enough away from the house—and fast.

The fairgrounds were about an hour away by bike, but

Gabby made it halfway there in fifteen minutes. By then she was on a major road lined with swaths of verdant lawn. Beyond the grass sat wide sidewalks abutting coffee shops, upscale clothing stores, specialty markets, and outdoor cafés. It was the kind of place people would park their cars, then wander the sidewalks, shopping and grazing.

In other words, it was the kind of area where G.E.T.O.U.T. couldn't grab Sharli without causing a major scene. Gabby slowed her speed and tried to take deep breaths. The breaths caught in her throat and made her cough.

"Why'd you slow down?" Petey shouted from his bag at the front of the bike. "Faster, faster!"

"Fah-tah!" Sharli echoed from the baby seat behind Gabby.

Sneakers was the only one who looked happy to take it down a notch. He adjusted his gait to a light trot and seemed to smile.

"We're going fast enough," Gabby told the kids. "We'll be there in a little while."

A car beeped behind her. Gabby veered closer to the road's wide shoulder, expecting the car to zoom past her. Instead she heard it slow down.

Gabby's heart thudded. Could it be G.E.T.O.U.T.? Did they see her leaving with Sharli? Had they been tailing her all this time? Gabby instinctively reached out to adjust the rearview mirror she'd mounted on her left handlebar, but this was Blinzarra's bike. The mirror wasn't there.

Suddenly, an image filled her head: the front end of a sparkling-clean silver SUV. Its driver was late-middle-age, but TV-doctor-good-looking, with salt-and-pepper hair, and eyes so blue their color shone through the windshield.

The license plate on the front of his car said SLVR FAHX.

Gabby shook her head, hard. She'd never had visions like these before today, and now she was on her third. Had Edwina done this to her? Did it happen in that weird dream-that-wasn't-a-dream last night? Had she zapped Gabby with some kind of power to help her succeed at this very important babysitting job?

Whatever it was, Gabby didn't like it. The visions were too jarring. They made her feel like someone else had grabbed the reins of her brain.

Part of her hoped this particular vision was all her imagination, and she'd turn to see nothing at all behind her. Unfortunately, that wasn't the case. The SUV was right there, and Arlington, a.k.a. the Silver Fox, a.k.a. Gabby's mom's recently reinstated boyfriend, was at the wheel. When he noticed Gabby looking at him, he smiled and waved, then pointed at the shoulder of the road, gesturing for her to pull over. With a sinking heart, she did as he asked.

68

"Why are we stopping?" Petey called from his bag. "I wanna get to the fair!"

Gabby hopped off the bike, engaged the kickstand, then lunged forward and whisper-hissed to Petey. "Not a word. I know this guy. We can't let him see you."

"What guy? What's going on? I wanna come out and look."

The bag shifted around like Petey was about to make good on his threat, but the SUV had already pulled over in front of them and Arlington was getting out. Pulse racing, Gabby quickly flicked a finger against the bag to warn Petey to keep still.

"Ow!" he yelped, and Gabby smiled and said an absurdly loud "HI!" at the same time so Arlington wouldn't notice the squawk.

Arlington smiled back as he strode toward Gabby. His teeth were so white they were like a solar eclipse; Gabby couldn't look directly at them or they'd sear her eyes. He wore jeans and a tucked-in, button-down light blue top with a navy-blue blazer over it. He always looked like he was walking through the middle of a pharmaceutical ad—the kind they aired during the cooking shows Gabby watched with her mom. Maybe that's why Alice liked him so much—from the start, he'd looked familiar to her.

"Your favorite license plate, right?" he asked, gesturing

back to SLVR FAHX, which was on the back of his car as well as the front. Gabby forced herself not to grimace. Arlington had overheard Zee and Gabby calling him "Silver Fox" and took it as a compliment.

It wasn't.

"Silver Fox" had been their code name for him long before he was Alice's boyfriend, back when he was just a suspicious stranger who seemed far too interested in Gabby and her babysitting schedule. They'd been sure he was an agent for G.E.T.O.U.T., and equally positive he had only started dating Alice to get closer to Gabby's secrets. Of the zillion reasons Gabby was so happy her dad had come back into their lives, getting rid of Arlington had been in her top ten; the worst part of her parents splitting up had been his return.

Gabby didn't trust Arlington. She knew now that he didn't work for G.E.T.O.U.T.—Edwina had checked for her. But Edwina had also discovered he'd been off-planet at some point in his life. It was fishy, just like it was fishy the way he tried to kiss up to Gabby and Carmen, doing things like getting that license plate he thought Gabby would like. Or the way he asked too many questions about Gabby's babysitting jobs and always pushed to see if he and Alice could "pop by" while she was working.

If the Silver Fox made her mom happy, fine. But Gabby

herself tried to stay as far away from him as possible, and she *definitely* kept the kids she babysat out of his sight.

Until now.

"What a cutie!" he said, leaning over Sharli's seat and tickling her under her chin.

Sharli giggled and kicked happily, but her eyes were on the car keys he held in his other hand. Arlington didn't notice as they floated out of his grip, higher . . . higher . . .

"Sharli!" Gabby cried excitedly, getting the toddler's attention. Arlington's keys instantly crashed to the ground.

"Oops," Arlington said. "Dropped these."

When he bent to pick them up, Gabby gave Sharli a pleading look and shook her head the littlest bit. She doubted the *Please don't move things with your mind* message was clear, but she had to try.

"I'm surprised you're working on fair day, Gabby," Arlington said as he stood up. "I know your mom could use your support."

Gabby's jaw tensed, and her hand drifted up to the chain around her neck. It held her dad's dog tags. She still wore them under her shirt, even though he'd come home. She'd offered to give them back, but her dad had said he was honored that Gabby had worn them in his absence, and he wanted her to keep them.

If her *dad* had said Alice needed Gabby's support that

would be fine, but if the Silver Fox thought for a second that he knew better than her what Alice needed, he was out of his mind. Besides, Gabby already knew Alice needed her. She felt guilty enough about ditching without Arlington rubbing it in.

"Mom understands when I have a job," Gabby said tightly. "But it all worked out because I'm taking the kids to the fair right now."

"Kids?" Arlington laughed. "You're counting the dog?"

Actually, she'd been counting Petey. She was furious at herself for making a mistake like that in front of Arlington, but at least he'd shown her exactly how to cover it up.

"Yes," she said quickly. "Totally counting the dog. Good to see you—gotta go."

"Wait!" he said. "I'm going to the fair, too. Let me take you."

Alarm bells screamed in Gabby's head. She and Satchel had seen a lot of horror movies, and she'd learned a lot of things. Among those at the top of the list were *Never split up*, *Never be in a group of teenagers in a remote location*, and *Never get in a car with someone suspicious*. If Arlington had been waiting all this time to get his hands on an alien, this would be the perfect way to do it.

Then she gasped out loud. What if *Arlington* was behind

Edwina's warning? What if he was involved with whoever was after Sharli and Blinzarra?

"You okay?" he asked. His eyes crinkled suspiciously.

"Fine!" Gabby said quickly. She pushed up her kickstand and straddled the bike. "And a ride would be great, but I can't take it. You don't have a toddler seat in your car."

"Actually, I do." Arlington touched his key fob, and his trunk popped open. Inside the otherwise spotless expanse sat an infant seat and a child booster seat. "For when my niece and nephew visit."

In all the time she'd known him, this was the first she'd heard about a niece and nephew. Her whole body broke out in nervous sweat.

"Cool!" she said. "But . . . I have the bike. It wouldn't fit in your trunk."

Arlington smiled. He leaned over, reaching back into his trunk . . . and his phone rose out of his back pocket and danced in midair.

Gabby turned around to see Sharli had leaned over in her seat. She smiled and waved as she made the phone pirouette. Gabby moved to block her view of the phone, but Sharli quickly leaned the opposite way so she could still see it.

This happened several times in a single second, and Sharli squealed out loud, loving this new game.

"Here we go," Arlington said.

He was about to turn around and see his phone defying gravity.

Gabby leaped off the bike, threw down the kickstand, and charged Arlington, purposely smacking his back as she swatted the phone to the ground.

"Huge bug on your back!" she explained as he spun around to face her. "Giant. Super-scary. Oops, I think I knocked your phone out of your pocket. Sorry."

"That's okay," he said, but he sounded dubious. He kept his eye on Gabby as he knelt to pick it up.

Gabby peeked. The screen wasn't cracked. Whew. She'd have felt bad if it was.

"Bike rack," he said, gesturing to a metallic bracket that had been hidden behind the car seats. "So we're set. Wanna put the car seat in the back? I'll grab the baby."

"NO!"

Gabby screamed loud enough to make people all the way across the lawn at a sidewalk cafe turn and stare. She acknowledged them with a nod and a wave, and Arlington turned red.

"Sorry," Gabby said, her mind racing. "It's just . . . your car is so clean. And Sneakers sheds. A lot. All over the place."

"That's okay," Arlington said. "I can always vacuum. Come on, Sneakers. Let's get you in the car."

Arlington walked to the spaniel. In two seconds Sneakers would be in his arms and Gabby would have no choice but to pile in after him—*after* she secretly got Petey out of his bag and hidden in her knapsack. Maybe it would be fine and Arlington would just drive them to the fair, but if he didn't . . .

Gabby saw it so clearly in her mind: Arlington locking the doors and taking them far away, maybe to some hideous lab where he'd run evil experiments on Sharli—and Petey, too, when he found him. And then—

The snarling and growling was so ferocious, Gabby yelped out loud. She immediately turned to the sidewalk, positive that some shopper had lost control of a vicious guard dog. Then she heard Arlington cry out, "Whoa!" and realized the horrible, guttural noise was coming from Sneakers. He lunged and snapped at Arlington, baring his teeth and barking and growling with such fervor that spittle flew from his snout.

"How does that dog live with children?!" Arlington cried as he pressed himself back against his car. "He's dangerous!"

"He's not, though," Gabby said, flustered. "He hasn't been." Then she turned to the dog as if she could ask him for an explanation and get one in return. "Sneakers?"

The minute Gabby said his name, Sneakers snapped back to himself. He stopped barking, sat, and wagged his tail.

Every sign of menace was so far gone, it was impossible for Gabby to believe she'd even seen it.

"I think you should call your client and tell them you can't watch that dog," Arlington said. He was leaning against the back of his car now, his face ashen. "You could get hurt."

Gabby knelt down and looked at Sneakers, confused. The dog trotted to her, put his front paws around Gabby's neck in a big hug, and licked her face.

"He's really sweet to me," Gabby said. She offered up the only explanation she could think of. "Maybe he had a bad experience with men and doesn't like them. I'm sorry. I guess we'll just meet you at the fair."

Arlington pursed his lips as if he didn't like that idea, but he nodded. "Yeah. Okay. Yeah. I'll see you there. Ride safe, all right?"

"I will."

Gabby kept petting Sneakers as Arlington closed up his trunk, got into his car, and drove away. Then she leaned forward so she was nose-to-snout with Sneakers and rubbed his head. "You are a good, good dog," she said. "And smart, too. You could tell I didn't want us to go with him, couldn't you?"

"Can I stop being quiet now?" Petey called from the basket. "That took *forever*! I wanna get to the fair!"

Gabby peeked toward the sidewalk to see if anyone had noticed her bicycle bag talking to her, but everyone was still window shopping, sipping coffee, and otherwise minding their own business. Even the people closest to Gabby, at the three tables outside the café directly across the lawn from her, stayed focused on one another and their meals.

Still, better to be careful. Gabby leaned close to the bag and spoke softly. "I was thinking, maybe we should go somewhere else, instead of the fair. Like the mall, or the park."

Anywhere without the Silver Fox, she thought. But she didn't want Petey to know they might be in any kind of danger.

"No! The fair! You promised!"

"Actually, I'm pretty careful about the word 'promise,' and I—"

"Sharli, do you want to go to the fair?"

"FAH!"

"And what if Gabby says no?"

Sharli didn't respond. She scrunched up her face and pooked out her lip like she was about to cry, then turned to look across the lawn. Customers at all three café tables gaped as their coffee cups and plates of food levitated into the air.

"Whoa, whoa, whoa!" Gabby said. She leaped in front of Sharli and bobbed and weaved, eager to cut off her view. "Okay, the fair, we're going."

Behind her, Gabby heard the *CLANK* of plates dropping

back onto metal tables and surprised squeals as food and hopefully-not-too-hot coffee splashed onto people's laps.

In other circumstances, Gabby would run over to help clean up and make sure everyone was okay. Right now, however, she had two alien kids whose lives would be at risk if they were discovered, and who were exponentially more likely to give themselves away every second they weren't at the fair.

She hopped back on the bike and pedaled even faster than before.

chapter EIGHT

"I hear music!" a voice screamed. "I smell popcorn! And cotton candy! And animal poop! We're at the fair!"

It sounded like Petey was right by Gabby's ear . . . but that was impossible.

Then Sneakers barked, and Gabby saw what Petey had done, as if it was happening right in front of her. His bag unzipped, then he climbed out and held onto the zipper tab to swing around the bike, where he curled his arms and legs around the frame, slid down it, then bounced off the empty water-bottle holder, using the bracket like a trampoline.

He somersaulted through the air, then gripped the back of Gabby's puffy purple jacket, which he climbed until he sat on her left shoulder, perched like a parrot.

Gabby's heart stopped a million times as the vision played; when it ended she was breathless. She really had to tell Edwina to take away this power. It wasn't helping her babysitting skills, and it was *definitely* bad for her stress levels.

Even though she'd heard him speak right into her ear, she reached up to her shoulder to make sure Petey was really there.

"Cut it out!" Petey wailed. "If you tickle me, you'll make me fall."

"*I'll* make you fall? Why did you unbuckle? It's not safe!"

"I know what I'm doing," Petey said. "And Sneakers would've caught me if I fell. Come on—let's go see everything!"

With Petey out of his basket and therefore shockingly unsafe, Gabby was eager to pull into one of the many bike racks in the fairgrounds' giant paved parking lot. It was only after she did, then quickly texted Zee and Satchel to let them know where she was, that she remembered something.

"Shoot, I don't have a lock. I can't just leave the bike here."

Sneakers whined and pawed at a small bag on the back

of the bike, just under the seat. Gabby unzipped it and found a thick, coiled bike chain and a lock with a key.

"So that's settled, then," Gabby said. "You're an alien dog, who understands every word I say. And you're a very good boy." She scratched Sneakers behind his ears, then chained the bike, snapped the lock shut, and put the key in a secret pocket on the very top of her knapsack.

"Come on, come on, come *on*!" Petey said. Gabby winced as he climbed up her curls and scampered over her scalp. "I wanna go in!"

"I'm thinking we should talk about personal space," Gabby said, trying to peer up into her hair. "Maybe ask before you start climbing someone's head."

Sharli held out her arms. "In! In! In!"

Sneakers barked and wagged his tail.

"Okay, we're going," Gabby relented, "but we need to blend in. So, Sharli, please don't move anything without touching it, okay?" She reached up and took Petey out of her hair, bringing him down to face her. "And, Petey, you can't let anyone see you. You can hide in my pocket, or—"

"Or in Sneakers's vest pockets, or behind your hair, or behind Sharli's braids . . ." Petey rolled his eyes as he rattled off the options. "I get it. I'm human-years ten. It's not like this stuff's new."

"Gabs!"

Gabby grinned and looked up to see her two best friends approaching. Zee was in the lead. She wore denim overalls as always, the pockets bursting with the zillion odds and ends she used to make her mechanical creations. Her blonde braids bounced and clacked as she ran, which made Sharli shake her own head of braids and giggle.

Right behind her loped Satchel. He was a good head taller than Gabby. He would have been even taller if he ever stood up straight, but he'd gotten so tall so young that he always sloped his shoulders to try to blend in. By now it was second nature. Satchel was all long limbs and bony joints, with a sharp nose that poked out behind the shock of black hair that fell in his face.

Gabby was thrilled to see them both.

"HEY!" she cried as Zee tackled her in a hug. Gabby hugged her back, keeping Petey clutched gently in one hand.

It was a bad idea. Petey quickly squirmed out of her grip and grabbed on to Zee's braids.

"Tiny person!" Satchel shouted, reeling back like he'd run into a glass wall. "In your hair! *Tiny person!*"

Satchel and Zee had both known about Gabby's alien babysitting adventures for a long time now, and Satchel had seen all kinds of otherwise inexplicable things, including the inside of a spaceship hurtling through outer space. He was totally on board to help with things like the pizza-dough breadsticks, and was always there in an instant if Gabby needed him, but he was much happier when he didn't have to *see* the impossible. It scared him, and Satchel preferred scary things to stay on TV or movie screens.

Zee, however, relished every opportunity to see an alien. "Where?" she said, and whipped her head around so quickly that Petey lost his grip on her braids and flew straight for Satchel. Reacting on instinct, Satchel reached out and caught him, but he was so freaked out that he juggled Petey up and down, making the boy's voice shake.

"I'm gonna hurl!" Petey cried.

"Satch, stop," Gabby said. Then she turned to Sharli. "Forget what I said before. Can you bring him to me?"

"YAH!" Sharli cried happily. She leaned forward in the bike seat and stared at Petey, who flew out of Satchel's hands and soared full speed into Gabby's stomach. Gabby doubled over with a low *oof* as Petey ricocheted off her and fell, but Sneakers darted in front of her and Petey landed safely on his back.

"Thanks, Sneakers," Petey said. Then he looked up at all of them indignantly. "Not a Nerf ball! Actual alien being here!"

"Sorry, Petey," Gabby said, her eyes darting around the parking lot. It was dotted with people, but they were all striding toward the fairgrounds entrance and seemed to have no interest in Gabby and her friends. "Just . . . maybe don't shout the 'alien' part out in public."

"Dude!" Zee enthused, her eyes sparkling. "That baby moved the tiny kid with her *mind*!"

"Toddler, yes," Gabby said. "Sharli, this is Zee and Satchel. Zee and Satch, this is Sharli and Petey. And Sneakers, the dog."

She left out the "most-likely-an-alien" from Sneakers's description. Less to explain that way.

"Sneakers!" Satchel cried. Within seconds he was on his knees, rubbing the dog behind his ears as the spaniel wagged his tail and covered Satchel's face with wet tongue-kisses.

"Ew," Petey grimaced from his spot on Sneakers's back. "Gross."

"I'm with the mini-kid," Zee said.

"Minisculean," Petey noted.

"Whatever," Zee said. "That thing licks its butt with that tongue. It's nasty."

"That *thing*?" Satchel said when Sneakers's snout was away from his mouth. "How do you not like dogs *or* babies?"

"Neither one of them can tell me what they want," Zee said. "I like things that can talk to me. Like robots. Or select people, but only if they aren't annoying."

"Yeah!" Petey cried. "No dogs or babies or annoying people! They're all too big anyway. Now let's go to the fair!" He ran to the top of Sneakers's head, then jumped into Satchel's hair, causing Satchel to spring to his feet and launch Petey into the air, where he grabbed one of the many cords spilling out of the pocket of Zee's overalls, swung back and forth to gain momentum, then launched himself onto her shoulder.

"Nice moves, Petey," Zee said. "Let's fair it."

"Wait," Gabby said. She took off Sharli's helmet and hooked it onto the bike, then unstrapped the little girl from her seat and settled her against her hip. "Okay, let's go. Petey, you've gotta stay hidden. Satch, can you take Sneakers?"

"Yeah! High five, Sneakers!"

Sneakers raised a paw and tapped Satchel's outstretched hand, then Satchel kissed the top of the spaniel's head and took his leash. Getting through the main gates took no time at all—Zee and Satchel had already been inside, so they just showed their hand stamps. Children under four were free, as were dogs, and while Gabby knew it would be the right thing to pay for Petey, she couldn't very well keep him a secret if she were buying him a ticket, so she only bought one for herself.

Once they were in, Gabby's mood soared like a balloon. There was so much to see! She was wide-eyed as they walked the midway, past its barkers hawking games—"Jug Toss!" "High Striker!" "Ring the Bottle!"—and foods that made no sense, but sounded too good to miss. "Hot Beef

Sundae!" "Giant Deep Fried Gummy Bear on a Stick!" "Donut Burger!" Beyond the midway she could see the tops of roller coasters and a Ferris wheel and a giant pirate ship that zipped in and out of her field of vision as it zoomed up and down. Gabby wanted to do everything all at once, and she could see Satchel, Zee, and Sharli felt the same way. Even Sneakers looked excited; his tail had perked up and he pranced along, sniffing at everything in the air.

Best of all, the fair was filled with people. It was the perfect place to hide in plain sight from whoever was after Sharli.

"I wanna do *all* the rides!" Petey cried. His voice was right in Gabby's ear. He'd made his way back to Gabby's shoulder again, though Gabby had no idea how or when.

"You're supposed to stay hidden." Gabby spoke softly, but it wasn't necessary. The fair throbbed with noise from screams, laughter, the *WHOOSH* of rides, and the constant blare of pop music from a zillion speakers.

"I *am* hidden!" Petey insisted. "Your hair's a big, curly mop. I could hide Sneakers in here with me."

"What do we do first, Gabs?" Zee asked. "Food? Tilt-A-Whirl? Or I've got some lenses in here," she added, rummaging in her deep side pockets. "I could rig up a microscope and check out a strand of Petey's hair. . . ."

86

"Let's go see my mom," Gabby said. "She'll want to know I'm here. Then we can check out everything else."

Together, the six of them walked through the midway, then turned left, away from the rides and toward the farm area. Here the smells changed from sugar, spices, and deep-fried everything to hay, musk . . . and a slight tinge of poop. Large, open pens held every farm animal imaginable: cows, sheep, giant hogs, horses, and even alpacas. Gabby held Sharli in her arms to make the long walk easier, but the little girl nearly hurled herself free, reaching out and calling to each one. "Oink, oink! Baaaaa! MOOOOOO!"

Gabby laughed. "Don't worry, we'll see them in a minute."

Beyond the farm animals stood the picnic area—a large field dotted with tables and benches, where scattered families shared meals from coolers they'd brought for the occasion. Most of the area was quiet, except for a single patch of lawn that bustled with life. There, a pop-up kitchen area filled with ovens, giant counters, and cabinets held the swarm of local chefs who'd spend the whole day working to create the world's largest pizza. A massive section of field had been cordoned off to hold the finished pie, which would need a diameter of at least one hundred and thirty-two feet to take the prize.

Gabby craned her neck to see between the crowd of onlookers and found Alice among the throng of chefs. The day had only begun, but already Alice's perfectly ironed hair stood out in flyaway wisps, and her brow was beaded with sweat as she threw her entire body into ferociously kneading a mound of dough as big as Sharli.

"Swear to everything, if she sweats into the pizza dough, I'm gonna yak," Zee said.

"Mom!" Gabby called, but Alice didn't even look up. Carmen, however, did. She was sitting away from the bustle on her favorite folding chair under an umbrella, both of which Alice had brought along for her comfort. Carmen wasn't interested in the fair itself—too noisy and too many people—and she'd never put up with sitting at a picnic table all day. The chair and a tablet loaded with e-books would keep her happy.

"She won't hear you, Gabby," she called. "And you can't have a dog near people cooking. It's unsanitary."

"But Sneakers is so sweet," Gabby said. She put Sharli down so the girl could toddle on the grass, then took Sneakers's leash. "Come on, Sneakers. Let's sniff the pizza."

Gabby couldn't hide her grin as she walked toward the chefs. She had no intention of letting Sneakers sniff the pizza, but she knew the idea of it would make Carmen crazy.

"Gabby, stop," Carmen said flatly. But when Gabby and

Sneakers kept striding forward, her voice got more frantic. "Gabby, come on! Gabby, *stop*! GABBY!"

Two people from the crowd turned at the sound of her name. Neither was Alice, and both made her regret ever setting foot in this part of the fair.

chapter
NINE

"Gabby Duran!"

Dina Parker, the reporter, lit up so brightly at the sight of Gabby that for a second Gabby thought the woman might actually be an incandescent alien. She flashed Gabby a megawatt smile, then glared at her cameraman, smacked his arm, and jerked her head. A second later she was all smiles again as they both strode Gabby's way.

"Gabby?" came another voice.

Gabby knew that one, too. The Silver Fox looked

confused as he broke from the crowd and walked toward her, his eyebrows furrowed at Sneakers.

Gabby smiled, but her insides churned. From a distance her hair hid Petey perfectly, but if Dina and Arlington were up close looking for aliens, they'd spot him in a second. Without moving her lips, Gabby whisper-hissed, "Petey, you gotta go. Stay close, but *hide*!"

It was too late. Dina was just a few steps away. Gabby's heart thudded, but it blended in with the thunder of running footsteps behind her.

"Gabs!" Zee shouted. "You can't talk to a big-time TV reporter with your hair like that! Turn around and let me fix it."

With a rush of relief, Gabby turned. She mouthed "Thank you" as Zee moved in close and reached up with one hand to pretend to fix Gabby's front curls. She didn't touch the back, which worked as a thick curtain to hide Petey while he jumped into the top pocket of Zee's overalls, which she'd emptied and now held open with her free hand. Once Petey was tucked safely inside, Zee darted away and Gabby turned back around to find Dina's perfectly painted face an inch from her own.

"Whoa!" Gabby said, backing away a step. "Hi."

"Well, hello," Dina said with a slow, lioness smile.

"Gabby," Arlington said as he pulled up next to Dina. He eyed Sneakers suspiciously, but the dog only sat and panted with a doggie smile. "I'm glad you made it." Then he squinted a bit and leaned around her. "But where's the baby?"

"A baby?" Dina asked excitedly. "You're watching a baby? Child of anyone my viewers would know?"

Gabby spun around and saw Sharli far across the field, toddling back toward the animals. Satchel was bent over, arms spread wide as he took tiny steps behind her, ready to catch her if she toppled. Zee—doubtless still hiding Petey—jogged toward them.

"Is that her?" Dina asked, following Gabby's gaze. Then she turned to her cameraman. "Let's go take a peek."

"Wait!" Gabby said, but Dina didn't listen. She trotted off toward Satchel and Sharli, moving remarkably well across the grass in her red high heels. Her lumbering cameraman followed, but his wide body and the large camera kept him several steps behind.

Gabby's mind raced. She'd had trouble with reporters before—babysitting celebrity kids meant paparazzi were always on the prowl. But while video of Adam Dent's kids was a problem, video of Sharli, or someone zooming in on video with Zee in it and seeing Petey, would be a disaster. As far as Gabby knew, Dina could be sending her videos directly to G.E.T.O.U.T. Gabby could imagine them swarming the fair, grabbing Sharli and Petey and—

Sneakers took off, yanking his leash free of Gabby's grip. He zipped in front of the cameraman, who lost his footing and splatted forward into the grass, the camera bouncing out of his hands. A nanosecond later, the dog reached Dina. Teeth bared and snarling, Sneakers snapped at her ankles, forcing her to stop in her tracks.

"Be careful! That dog is ferocious!" Arlington shouted, though Gabby noticed he made no move to help. He even backed away a few steps. Gabby, however, ran full tilt into the fray.

"Get away, get away, get away!" Dina squealed.

"Sorry," Gabby said, panting as she reached them and picked up Sneakers's leash. "He's really protective."

Gabby hadn't realized that Carmen had left her chair and made her way to the fracas until she spoke up.

"Excuse me," she said to Dina, "I notice you're over here, but you told my mother your job is to report on the world-record pizza, which is over *there*. Is something wrong?"

Gabby looked at her sister, small for her age, with her too-short straight-cut bangs and her inexpressive gaze. It seemed impossible that anyone would find her intimidating, but Gabby had seen grown-ups flounder time and again under Carmen's inscrutable stare, and Dina was no exception. She grimaced uncomfortably, then pulled herself tall, adjusted the jacket on her bright red pantsuit, tossed her hair, and flashed her camera-ready smile.

"Nothing's wrong," she said. "Nothing at all."

She turned on her heel and walked back toward the chefs, pausing as she met her cameraman on the way. "Did you get that dog attacking me?" she growled as he fell into step with her. "I want to take the video to animal control."

"No," the cameraman replied. "I fell, remember? You want me to get some footage of the dog?"

Dina turned around, but Sneakers had long since stopped barking. He sat calmly at Gabby's side, his tail thumping happily.

"Forget it," Dina said.

"Thanks, Car," Gabby said as Dina and her cameraman strode out of earshot.

"For what? I just wanted to know why she wasn't doing her job."

Gabby hugged Carmen anyway and smiled when her sister stiffened in her grip. "Tell Mom I'll do my best to come back for the judging," she said, though she knew she wouldn't go anywhere near the picnic area again as long as she was still with the kids.

"Wait," Carmen said. "I need a charger. Mom forgot to

bring one—even though I reminded her five-and-a quarter times—and my tablet's almost dead."

"Five-and-a-quarter times?" Gabby asked as she shrugged off her knapsack.

"The sixth time she cut me off two and half words into my sentence."

Gabby held out the charger she always kept in her knapsack. She didn't love being without it while she was working—especially when she needed to keep checking her phone for potential Edwina updates—but Carmen had just saved her butt from Dina, so it was the least Gabby could do. Plus, her own phone was at 97 percent battery; she'd be fine.

Gabby closed her fist around the charger. "Only if I get another hug."

Carmen sighed like the weight of the world was on her back. "Fine. But make it quick."

Gabby lifted her sister off the ground in a fierce bear hug that Carmen somehow managed to endure, then she gave her sister the charger and ran with Sneakers to catch up to Satchel and Zee. They were back in the Farm Zone, watching three large cows meander and graze. The cows were penned in by a horizontal-slat fence, and Satchel held up Sharli so she could stand on the middle slat and lean against the top.

"Check it out," Zee said when she saw Gabby. "Sharli's trying to move the cow."

Gabby scanned the pen nervously—was a cow off the ground?

"The brown-and-white one," Satchel said, and the lock of hair in his face flopped as he nodded across the pen. Gabby didn't see anything strange, until she noticed the cow's udder. It was smooshed to one side, and all the teats were pointed at Gabby and her friends, as if the udder were full of metal filings and Sharli held a giant magnet.

"I think the cow's too big for her," Satchel said softly. Then he raised his voice and singsonged so Sharli could hear. "Great try, though, Sharli! You're doing so good!"

"Cow!" Sharli said proudly, and clapped her hands.

"*Pfft,*" Petey said, and Gabby saw he was still in Zee's top pocket. If he had to, he could pass for a doll. "No she isn't. She's doing *zip.* The cow isn't moving at all."

Sharli shot him a look, then she stared back at the cow. A second later, one of the udders squeezed and shot a stream of milk right into Petey's face.

"Hey, come on!" he spluttered.

Zee laughed but stopped short when the milk dripped down over her overalls. "For real?! Now I'm gonna smell like sour cow!"

People were starting to stare. Gabby spun Zee away from the fence. "Come on, let's go see more animals."

As they moved toward the chickens, Gabby checked her phone. She wanted to make sure Edwina hadn't called. She didn't want to go back too early if it was still dangerous at Sharli's house, but she also didn't want to be out at the fair when Petey's dad and Blinzarra came home.

No messages. To be honest, Gabby was glad. She'd been looking forward to hanging out at the fair with Zee and Satchel for ages; seeing it with Sneakers, Sharli, and Petey only made it better. They checked out all the animal pens—the sheep, the pigs, the llamas—and Gabby was impressed that Sneakers didn't react to the other animals at all, except to wag his tail. A farmer even let Sneakers accompany the group into the petting zoo, and he adorably lay flat on the ground to get nose to nose with a bunny. When Sharli petted a sheep, Sneakers rubbed up against the sheep's other side, like he was petting it, too.

Petey also had a great time, especially when Zee snuck him out of her pocket and deposited him on a sheep's back. He sank deep into its coat and giggled out loud. "Gabby, the sheep's hair's just like yours!"

After visiting the animals, they went to the Ride Zone. Gabby, Zee, and Satchel all loved the highest, fastest, wildest rides, but Gabby was on duty, so if anyone was going to miss out, she knew it should be her. After she checked her phone to make sure there weren't any updates from Edwina, she made her decision: "You guys go," she told Zee and Satchel. "I'll stay with Sneakers, Petey, and Sharli."

"What?!" Petey complained. "I'm not a baby. I want to go on the big rides, too."

"You can't," Gabby said. "They don't have seat belts for you."

"'Cause they're size-ist!" Petey said. "But their prejudice shouldn't be my problem. I'll just sit in Zee's pocket. Or she can hold me really, really tight."

"Won't work, Petey-Man," Zee said. "Laws of physics. You'd fly out and splatter like a pancake."

"Ew," Satchel said. "And do pancakes really splatter? I mean, maybe if they're undercooked, then I guess the runny insides would splatter all over . . ."

"No runny insides," Gabby insisted, then she turned to Petey. "No dangerous rides."

"Hold up, Gabs," Zee said. "Gimme a sec."

She put Petey in one of Sneakers's vest pockets, then plopped down cross-legged right in the middle of the walk-way. Gabby and Satchel knew better than to bother her when inspiration hit, so they took Sneakers, Sharli, and Petey on the nearest kiddie ride—a train that went slowly around in a circle—while they waited.

Sharli loved it. Petey groused the whole time. When they got off, he was so happy to be free, he jumped out of Sneakers's pocket and darted into an empty paper soda cup someone had tossed on the ground. He ran inside the cup like it was a hamster wheel, rolling unseen right up to Zee.

"What'cha got?" he asked her as Gabby approached with the others.

"Your ticket to happiness," Zee crowed. She pulled open her top pocket. "Safety harness."

Gabby looked inside. She had no idea how Zee had done it, but somehow she'd wrangled the random items in her other pockets to create a full-body harness for a miniature kid. It looked like the restraints for a baby swing, blended with something a person would wear to go sky diving. There were straps for Petey's legs, plus an upper-body piece that folded down to let him get in, then zipped into place to hold him tight. When Petey slipped inside to try it, Gabby had to admit he looked even safer and more snug than he'd been inside his bike-bag seat. Still, she dragged Zee over to a patch of grass and made her run, jump, and do cartwheels with Petey inside to make sure he didn't fall out. She even had Zee unclip the top of her overalls and shake the bib part as hard as she could to ensure Petey didn't budge.

He didn't. Not even a bit.

"That was *awesome*!" he crowed when Zee clipped back up. "Now to the Danger Drop!"

The Danger Drop took its riders thirty feet straight into the air, then let them freefall back down. Gabby had visions of runny pancake insides, and her stomach turned.

"Maybe work your way up to the Danger Drop," she said.

"Deal," Satchel said. "We'll start on the Scrambler. I promise I won't let Zee smush him."

"I would never smush him," Zee said. "I mean, not on purpose."

Gabby almost called the whole thing off and kept Petey on the kiddie rides, but she knew she could count on Satchel to be careful, plus Zee had mad construction skills and understood the laws of physics well enough to bend them into submission. Her pride alone would keep Petey safe; Zee would never allow one of her inventions to be the reason anyone got hurt.

The fair was amazingly cool about bringing dogs on kiddie rides, so Gabby took Sneakers and Sharli, while Petey went off with Zee and Satchel. Satchel took selfies of their group after each ride and sent them to Gabby to prove they were still alive. Gabby appreciated it, but she also promptly deleted each one and made them do the same. After so much time as an A.L.I.E.N. associate, she'd learned that nothing on anyone's cell phone was truly safe. That said, Petey looked deliriously happy in each picture, and Sneakers and Sharli were loving their rides, too. Gabby wondered if they'd ever been to a fair before. Would Blinzarra have taken Sharli last year? Did Petey's parents ever find a way to take him?

Gabby doubted it. There was something about the way Sharli's eyes lit up at every ride, and how she kept taking Gabby's hand and pulling her back in line saying, "'Gen! 'Gen! Peeeeez!" Even the way Sharli giggled as her braids clickety-clacked in the breeze while the kiddie coaster chugged along its track—it all seemed new to her, and Gabby was thrilled to give her the experience.

They spent ages exhausting every ride in the kiddie area multiple times over. Gabby had so much fun, she almost forgot that the fair wasn't her original plan, and she was only there because of some kind of emergency. Each time she did remember it was like an electric shock through her spine and she'd quickly whip out her phone to check for texts from Edwina, but there was nothing.

Was that good? Was it bad? Gabby had no way to know. All she could do was follow Edwina's orders in the text she'd sent: *Act naturally, and await further instructions.*

So that's what she'd do.

After a couple of hours, Gabby knew Sharli and Sneakers needed food, so she texted Satchel and Zee to meet her at the top of the midway. Gabby got there first, and she tried to keep Sharli entertained by letting her watch the carnival games. Sharli wasn't so interested in the games, but she went wild for the prizes. "Bear!" she squealed. "Big bear! Sharli big bear!"

"I'll try to win you a big bear, Sharli," Satchel offered as he and Zee joined them. Petey was out of his harness but still inside Zee's top pocket so he could easily duck out of sight.

Gabby was beyond relieved to see them. She had to use the bathroom, and it'd be much easier to do that solo than with Sharli and Sneakers in tow. With human three-year-olds she'd take them along anyway just to make sure they had the opportunity, but Blinzarra had said her and Sharli's bodies didn't work that way. She didn't know about Petey and Sneakers, but Petey was old enough to speak up for himself, and Sneakers had shown he was smart—if he needed it, he'd lead them to a place where he could do his business. She gave Sneakers's leash to Satchel, had Sharli take his other hand, then she shrugged off her purple knapsack and got out some money, which she gave to Zee.

"Nice!" Zee said. "For games?"

"For food," Gabby said. A.L.I.E.N. babysitting jobs paid

ridiculously well, and while she was saving most of what she earned for R.A.M.A., the Royal Academy for the Musical Arts and her future college of choice, she kept a small amount handy for unexpected expenses on the job.

"Got it. Food. And maybe one or two games." Zee knelt down to meet Sharli's eyes. "'Cause Satchel could try, but I bet *you'd* win us the *biggest* bear!"

"That's cheating, Zee!" Gabby called, but she was already walking away. She couldn't wait any longer, especially since the closest bathrooms were alllll the way down the midway. When she finally made it there, she had to wait in a line so long she had to play every note of *En Forêt* by Eugéne Bozza—the hardest piece of French horn music she knew—in her head just to distract her from the urgency. Twenty minutes went by before she got to a stall, and she must have been delirious from the wait because the whole time she was inside, she had bizarre flashes of the fairgrounds, like she was seeing them right in front of her eyes. She saw the midway rushing by, as if she were running quickly right up the main drag. . . .

Then it disappeared and she was back in the stall. Moments later it happened again. She saw a quick flash of people walking past the Ring Toss game, looking down at her as they came her way, walking in the opposite direction . . . then it was gone.

Gabby's skin prickled. She didn't like this new power Edwina had given her one bit, but the visions never came for no reason. Every time they'd shown her something she needed to see.

So why did she need to see these flashes of the fair?

Gabby had no idea, but she had a terrible feeling she had to get back to Sharli, Sneakers, and Petey as soon as possible.

She hurried out of the stall and washed her hands in record time, then pushed her way through the crowds around the door, only to reel back as she had another flash, this time of the Ride Zone moving swiftly past her, as if she were at a jog. The vision disappeared as fast as it came, but it left Gabby breathless. She yanked out her phone and texted Zee and Satchel: *All OK? Ready to meet back up. Where are you?*

The reply from Zee came back right away: *LOL—same place as when u left us 5 mins ago! Giant Deep-Fried Gummy Bear on a Stick!!!*

Gabby's skin tingled and her ears burned.

She hadn't been at Giant Deep-Fried Gummy Bear on a Stick five minutes ago. She'd been in a bathroom stall five minutes ago.

Something was wrong. Very wrong.

Another vision hijacked her brain: the kiddie ride area,

with lots of people walking by. In the vision Gabby looked up at them from knee level.

It faded right away, but Gabby's pulse rushed in her ears as she understood.

The vision was from a person's *knee level*—the way *Sneakers* would see everything.

Instantly, Gabby remembered every moment she'd seen a flash of something she couldn't see: Petey making faces at Sharli, Petey landing on Sneakers's fur, the Silver Fox's SUV driving up behind her. She hadn't imagined them, and it wasn't that Edwina had given her some kind of sixth sense to help her be a better babysitter.

Sneakers had seen them and sent them into her head.

And now Sneakers was moving quickly through the fairgrounds, while Zee and Satchel were in line for giant deep fried gummy bears on a stick.

Heart pounding out of her chest, Gabby wheeled around until she saw a smiling giant red cardboard gummy bear rising from a stand across the midway.

She broke into a run.

chapter
TEN

"Zee!" Gabby screamed as she ran toward the Giant Deep-Fried Gummy Bear stand, dodging and darting around swarms of fair-goers on her way. "Satchel!"

She found them at the front of the line. Zee was just reaching out to receive five giant, sort-of-bear-shaped, dough-crusted, and sugar-dusted deep fried blobs on sticks, while Satchel waited just behind her. He bowed under the weight of a massive stuffed bear, holding it like he was giving it a piggy back ride.

Aside from that, they were alone.

"Gabs, I know you said you didn't want one of these, but trust me, you do," Zee said.

Satchel looked up at Gabby from under the bear and frowned. "Where are Sneakers and the kids?"

Gabby's heart dropped into her stomach. She'd had a terrible feeling this was coming, but hearing him say the words was much, much worse.

"I don't have them," she said. "You said in your text I was here five minutes ago, but I wasn't. I haven't seen you since I left for the bathroom."

Zee wrinkled her face. "That's not true. You were just here. You said you wanted to get the kids real food before they had the gummy bears, so that's where you took them."

Gabby shook her head. "It wasn't me."

"It had to be you," Zee said. "I mean, it was *you*. It was exactly you!"

"Unless it was a Body Snatcher!" Satchel said, his eyes wide. "Oh snap! An alien Body Snatcher took Sneakers and the kids!"

In other circumstances, Gabby would have been impressed that Satchel had come to this conclusion without losing consciousness or having his brain explode, but right now she was too worried to even think about that.

The kids were *gone*, taken away by someone who could change their shape to look exactly like her, and the only clue they had was . . .

Gabby put her hand to her head as she had another vision. She saw the fair from Sneakers's point of view again. Everything bounced up and down, as if he were moving at a trot. The Danger Drop loomed ahead in the distance. . . .

And then the vision was gone.

"This way!" Gabby said, and ran top speed back up the midway. Zee and Satchel raced to catch up with her, Zee still clutching a fistful of giant deep-fried gummy bears on a stick, Satchel still holding the massive stuffed bear on his back.

"Where are we going?" Satchel asked, although since he was bent over, the stuffed bear's head was closer to Gabby's, and it looked like it was the one talking to her.

"Sneakers isn't just a dog," Gabby panted as she ran. "He's an *alien* dog, and he's sending me images of where they are. They're headed for the Danger Drop!"

"They're going on a ride?" Zee asked, then took a big bite of deep-fried gummy bear on a stick.

"Dunno," Gabby said. She was running so fast she could barely get the word out, but Zee didn't seem winded at all. She took another big bite of gummy bear and Gabby gaped. "How can you eat right now?"

"What am I gonna do, waste 'em? Besides, instant energy. Here."

She held out a stick to Gabby, but Gabby shook her head. She had a cramp, and she knew no matter how fast she ran, she'd never catch up with whoever had Sneakers and the kids—not when they had such a huge head start.

"Daaaaad!" a little girl whined. She was several yards ahead of Gabby, Zee, and Satchel, but her voice was so loud and screechy it cut through everything. "I told you, I want a bear like that! You proooomised!"

Gabby looked. The girl was around six years old. She was sitting on her father's lap, and her father was riding in a mobility scooter—a small motorized vehicle the fair rented out to people who had the ability to walk but were uncomfortable doing so for the amount of time it took to tackle an entire fair day. This particular dad looked around the same age as the Silver Fox, albeit not quite as fit. He also looked exhausted, and while that might have been from negotiating the crowds all day, Gabby had a feeling the whining had a lot to do with it, too.

"I tried!" the dad snapped. "It's impossible. The games are rigged!"

"It's not fair!" the girl wailed. "I never get *anything*!"

Gabby couldn't help but notice the girl was holding a giant cotton candy, had a balloon-hat on her head, more balloons tied to her wrist, wore a fair-themed T-shirt, and had clearly just come from a face-painting booth, because her face looked like a bunny's. "*Daaaaaaaaad!!! I need a big big beeeeear!*"

As a babysitter, it was Gabby's policy not to give in to whining kids and their demands. This, however, was an emergency. She veered to the dad and spoke rapid-fire. "We'll give you the bear for the scooter."

"YES!" cried the little girl.

"What?!" Satchel said. "This is our bear."

"Deal!" the dad said, and in a fluid motion that belied his need for the scooter in the first place, he leaped to his feet, grabbed the giant stuffed bear, and handed it to his delighted daughter.

"I really liked that bear," Satchel said sadly, watching it go.

"No time," Gabby said. "On the scooter."

They all climbed onto the scooter, Gabby at the very front edge of the seat and Zee and Satchel perched on the sides. Then Gabby turned the speed knob and squeezed the hand control as hard as she could.

The scooter puttered along, barely faster than the three of them could walk.

"You made us give up the bear for this?!" Satchel wailed.

"Zee, what can you do?" Gabby asked.

"Give me thirty seconds," Zee said, already hopping off the scooter and reaching into her over-full pockets.

Gabby turned off the scooter and waited. She didn't look to see what Zee was doing; she knew she wouldn't have understood it anyway. Instead she drummed her fingers on the handlebars, counting off the seconds in her head. She was hoping for another vision from Sneakers, but nothing came.

Gabby had only reached "twenty-nine" when Zee leaped back onto the scooter.

"Gun it!" she said.

Keeping the speed knob all the way up, Gabby squeezed the hand control, and they rocketed forward. "WHOOOOOAAAAAH!!!!" they all wailed, which was good because it warned people to get out of their way. People jumped from the path, screaming and yanking their children to safety.

"Sorry, sorry, sorry!" Gabby cried, but she didn't dare slow down.

"There's a horn!" Satchel yelled. "My great-uncle Lou has one of these!"

"Where?!" Gabby asked.

Satchel didn't answer. He just leaned over Gabby and honked the horn again and again, a constant staccato blare that cleared a path far ahead of them. With no one in their way, Gabby felt better about her tenuous hold on the speeding scooter. It zoomed so quickly she couldn't keep the handlebars straight. The vehicle wavered from side to side, and Gabby was sure any bump in the path would roll them over.

Still, she didn't let up on the motor. She pushed it full force as they drove through the kiddie ride area, into the grown-up ride area, toward the Danger Drop. . . .

"There!" Zee cried, pointing up ahead. "It's you!"

"Oh snap!" Satchel exclaimed. "It's *all* of us!"

Gabby's jaw dropped open. That was a bad idea since she was speeding and the wind blew the ends of her hair inside her mouth, but she couldn't help it. Far ahead of her, Zee, and Satchel . . . were her, Zee, and Satchel. Gabby only saw them from the back, but she'd recognize them anywhere: Zee with her overalls and blonde braids; Satchel, taller and lanky, bent over in his slight hunch as he ran; and between them Gabby herself, with her purple knapsack, jeans, and long, curly hair. It was so obviously them that she had to take her eyes off the path for just a second to look down at herself, then to her left and right, to make sure they were also still *here*.

"I look weird when I run," Satchel said. "Do I really run like that?"

"We've got the kids," Zee said. "I mean, *they've* got the kids. I mean, *look*!"

She pointed, and Gabby saw what she meant. It was so jarring to see the carbon copy of her and her friends, she hadn't even paid attention to Sneakers, who was running with other-Satchel. This Satchel had pulled Sneakers's leash taut, so the dog had to crane his neck up as he ran, or else he'd choke. Other-Zee was holding Sharli—they could see the little girl's head through other-Zee's bouncing braids.

"And that's how you know it's not really us," Zee said. "I'd *never* be the one holding the kid."

"I don't know why Sneakers went along," Gabby said. "He barks and snarls when he doesn't like people. I've seen it."

"Maybe he wanted to protect Sharli and Petey," Satchel said. "If he fought, they might have kicked him away and left him behind. He sent you messages instead, like a good dog."

"Good *alien* dog," Zee said. Then she turned to Gabby and grinned. "Hey, maybe I can take him for a walk and pick up his poop! You'd let me have that sample, right?"

"Not the time, Zee!" Gabby said.

She was getting closer to the group, but she couldn't imagine where they were going. They'd passed the Danger Drop and were heading to the very edge of the fairgrounds, where the track of the Vertigo Vortex roller coaster bent closest to the ground. Beyond it there was nothing except a short field of grass, then a twenty-foot-high fence. If they got to the fence and split up, which way would Gabby go? Was Fake Alien Gabby holding Petey? Was Petey in Sneakers's vest pocket? Gabby couldn't tell. How could she possibly choose who to chase?

Gabby squeezed the hand control even tighter and the scooter gained more ground. She realized what she had to do. "I can get ahead of them," she said. "I'll ride circles around them so they can't get away, then I'll yell for Sneakers to attack. When he does, we grab Sharli and yell for Petey. He'll come out when we call him."

"We don't know where Petey is," Zee said. "What if he's tied up?"

"And what if Fake Alien Usses have laser vision and vaporize us?" Satchel cried.

"Or electro-lightning-bolt-vision," Zee said. "I totally want Fake Alien Me to have electro-lightning-bolt-vision. That's seriously cool."

"It's not cool if it kills us!" Gabby objected. "But it doesn't matter. We have to try it. We can't let them take the kids!"

Gabby leaned forward in her seat, staring daggers at her fake alien self as the space closed between them. Just a couple more yards and she'd pull ahead. The scooter wasn't wavering anymore. Gabby held it straight and true.

They were close now. A fifty-yard-dash away. Gabby

felt the hand control dig into the skin of her palm as she squeezed it tighter . . . tighter. . . .

Fake Alien Gabby turned around, and for one dizzying second, Gabby locked eyes with herself.

The impostor grimaced and turned her back on Gabby, digging something out of her jeans pocket. She threw it on the ground, and Gabby saw it land in the grass.

A second later a purple cone of light flashed, so bright that Gabby had to take her hands off the scooter controls to shield her eyes as she winced away. Behind her closed eyes, the negative image of the cone pulsed. Her eyes hurt, but she forced them open. The cone's after-image still blazed over everything she saw: the scooter, the bent-over figures of Zee and Satchel . . . but when she strained to see in front of her, no one was there. No Sneakers, no Sharli, no aliens in disguise. Nothing.

All she could make out was something pulsating in the grass. A small disc, blinking purple. Slowly at first, then faster and faster. Gabby didn't know what it meant, but she knew that was the last spot where she saw Sharli and Sneakers, and she had the horrible sensation that if that spot stopped flashing, she'd lose any chance to find them.

The spot blinked even faster, impossibly fast. Behind her Gabby vaguely heard Zee and Satchel, but it was like the sound came to her through water. All she saw was the purple blinking circle. It blinked at dizzying speed, and Gabby threw herself forward, sliding on the grass so she could touch it with her fingertips.

"GABBY!" Zee cried.

"NO!" Satchel yelled.

But all they could do was watch as their friend slipped impossibly inside the tiny circle and disappeared. By the time they raced to the spot, it was nothing but a smooth black rock.

chapter
ELEVEN

Gabby Duran had never been so comfortable in her life.

She was lying down. On a mattress, maybe? Whatever it was, she sank in just the right amount but also bobbed soothingly up and down, like the mattress was a raft on a gentle ocean. Her head was cradled on a thick, downy pillow. The sky above was cerulean blue, with puffy clouds that slowly wisped and reassembled to make bunnies, and snowflakes, and ice cream cones. Music played softly—Chopin's Nocturne in B-Flat Minor, op. 9, no. 1, which always made Gabby feel calm. She melted into her surroundings and had no sense of anything beyond this beautiful, relaxing, perfect moment in time.

Then two metallic hands smacked down on the horizon and a grinning copper-colored skull blotted out the sky.

Gabby screamed and bolted upright, but immediately banged her forehead on something hard.

"OW!" she yelled, holding a hand to her forehead as she fell back on the pillow.

She was encased in glass. Or plastic. Something totally clear but hard. She tilted her head down to get a better sense of her surroundings and saw she wasn't floating on an ocean at all. She was flat on her back on what looked like a hospital bed, but one with a nearly invisible dome over it, low enough that she couldn't sit up or roll over.

Her breath sped up, and she started to sweat as she realized she was basically in a particularly comfortable see-through casket.

The creature with the metal skull and hands—a robot, it had to be a robot—was still staring down at her. Gabby shouted to it as she pounded on the dome with her palms. "Hey! Get me out of here!"

The robot hissed and blurbled. It sounded like it was speaking to her, but it didn't move its mouth, and its expression didn't change.

Gabby shook her head. "I don't understand!" she shouted.

The robot slapped its hand to its forehead, and Gabby heard a loud *CLANK* as metal met metal. It lowered its arm out of Gabby's sight, then a second later she felt a kitten-tongue rasp against the back of her neck.

"Is that better?"

Nothing on the robot's grinning metallic skull moved, but it tilted its head questioningly, so Gabby assumed it—*he* (the voice sounded male)—was the one who asked her the question. In plain English now. Or to be more specific, remarkably fancy English. He spoke with an upper-crust British accent, and he raised his arms in a shrug as he asked, "Yes?"

"Um . . . yes," Gabby said.

"Good, good. My humblest apologies. Normally we let the Universal Translator—that raspy sensation you probably just felt on the back of your neck? We usually let that absorb into a visitor's skin the minute they arrive. It makes the entire process so much simpler. Please forgive me for my lapse, and I do hope it won't affect my rating on your consumer satisfaction survey."

"Okay," Gabby said. She wasn't afraid anymore, but she was definitely confused. "Um . . . where am I?"

"You're in a welcome pod," the robot said. "It's how we acclimate all non-native species to our planet. Interplanetary travel can be so disorienting otherwise, don't you find?"

"Inter . . . *planetary*?" Gabby asked.

The robot put its hands to either side of its head in a pantomime of shock. "I haven't shown you the welcome video! Oh, I am all discombobulated today. I'm so very sorry. Please do keep in mind these most humble apologies when you fill out that customer satisfaction survey."

The robot moved away, and the dome restricted Gabby's movement too much for her to follow where he went. The classical music in Gabby's ears suddenly stopped, replaced by a bouncy tune as red words in cheery bubble print appeared on the bright blue sky above her.

"Welcome to Mars!" An upbeat voice read the words out loud. "We're glad you came to visit, and hope you enjoy this video tour of our planet's highlights."

"Wait, what?!" Gabby banged on the dome. "*Mars?!*"

The robot's gruesome copper skull rose back into Gabby's field of vision. "Not *that* Mars," he said.

Gabby put the pieces together. Whatever "Mars" she was on, it was definitely another planet, and the only way she could have gotten here was by following her fake alien self through the blinking purple disc. That meant wherever she was, Sharli, Petey, and Sneakers were here, too.

The robot tried to duck away again as the narration continued, but Gabby pounded ferociously on the dome. "Stop! Turn the video off, please."

"Why?" he asked, worried. "Is it the narrator's voice? Is it not pleasant to you? Allow me to change it. Earthlings often find this one makes them quite happy."

A moment later, a deep, jolly voice filled Gabby's ears. "Ho-ho-ho! It's me, Santa Claus! And I'd like to welcome you to Mars! Not *that* Mars, of course—"

Gabby pounded on the dome again. "It's not the voice. Just please, let me out!"

Immediately, Santa's voice was cut off, the dome lifted, and Gabby sat up. As she did, the cushion underneath her sloshed and undulated. It was a water-mattress—that's why she'd felt like she was floating on the ocean. And her purple knapsack was sitting right at its foot. As she picked up her bag and slid it on, she realized the waterbed was just one item in what looked like an upscale hotel room. Nubby carpet lined the floor, recessed lighting gave the room a warm glow, and a small mahogany buffet table sat under a staggeringly large flat-panel TV. Through an open pocket door Gabby saw a bathroom with a deep claw-footed tub, a pedestal sink, and a rack filled with thick white towels. Only the bed's headboard seemed alien, blinking with digital read-outs in symbols Gabby couldn't understand.

"What *is* this place?" she asked the robot, who she now saw was around six feet tall. He was also Zee's robot dream come true. His copper joints were seamless. Top to bottom he had the sleek lines of a work of art. With the exception of his death mask of a face, he looked as if a flawlessly long and lithe humanoid body had been dipped in copper paint.

"As I said," the robot answered, "you *were* in a Welcome Pod, which is the main feature of our Mobile Holographic Acclimation Booth. I can tell you're agitated, and I do apologize. Our basic brain scans are usually quite adept at creating a comfortable transition from home planet to ours. Perhaps you'd like to freshen up in the bathroom? Or have a snack?"

He reached out and pressed a button on the buffet table and a panel slid open. Another panel rose to take its place, this one holding a silver platter filled with Pop-Tarts, fish sticks, and a bowl of maraschino cherries.

Gabby loved all these things. Turning them into a single meal was so brilliant, she was stunned she'd never done it herself. For a second she imagined tucking back into the water bed with the platter, turning on the TV, and seeing what was on. She had a strong suspicion she'd find all her favorite movies.

Under other circumstances it would have been tempting. At the moment she had far more important things to do.

"Just the way out, please," Gabby said.

"Are you sure?" the robot asked. "Because I have some wonderful brochures about the immediate vicinity. Mobile

Holographic Acclimation Booths appear wherever a traveler happens to arrive, and according to my records you rode the tail end of a portal-wave, which doesn't always have the most accurate aim. Perhaps a virtual hang-gliding tour would help you get your bearings. There's a lovely three-hour tour that comes with an impeccable lunch—"

"The way out," Gabby interrupted him. "Please."

While the robot's face didn't budge, he somehow managed to look crestfallen. Gabby felt bad for him, but she didn't have time for any kind of tour. She had to get out and start looking for Sharli, Petey, and Sneakers, especially if the robot was right about the purple light she rode here not having the best aim. She probably had some work ahead of her to find them.

Still, the robot looked awfully sad. And he really was trying hard to make things better for her.

"I promise I'll say nice things on my customer satisfaction survey," she said.

The robot perked up immediately. He stood taller, reached out to press what looked like a light switch on the wall, and a hatchway-shaped section of the wall shimmered. Gabby waited for it to disappear, but when it didn't she realized the shimmery section *was* the doorway—she just had to walk through.

"Thank you," she said. She started toward the hatch, then

doubled back and grabbed several Pop-Tarts and fish sticks. She wrapped them in two of the cloth napkins that had been folded like swans, then quickly shoved the parcels in her knapsack. Once she shrugged the knapsack back on, she popped a maraschino cherry in her mouth. "Thanks again!"

With a final wave, she strode through the hatchway.

She instantly wished she hadn't.

Strong winds buffeted her on every side. Red dirt kicked up and bit into her face, her hands, and every other sliver of her body that wasn't covered. Without thinking, she turned to walk back into the Mobile Holographic Acclimation Booth, but the entrance was gone. Nothing remained except a solid metal wall. Braving the harsh winds, Gabby staggered backward and shielded her eyes to look for another way in, but there was nothing. The booth was a simple steel cylinder, elegant and tapered at the bottom, and skinny enough that Gabby and one other person could have stood on either side and held hands around it. It was physically impossible that the large room with the bed and the buffet and the bathroom could have fit inside, but Gabby didn't have time to ponder the physics before her thoughts were interrupted by a massive *BOOM!*

In the near distance, the ground had become a dirt volcano, spewing red dust and rocks into the air.

She only had time to think the word "explosion" before another went off even closer.

Gabby quickly surveyed her surroundings. It might not have been "*that* Mars," but it certainly looked the way she imagined "that Mars" looked. All she could see were striated red rock mountains and boulders, all rising out of barren red dirt.

Another explosion went off, this one so loud she clapped her hands over her ears and ran, with no idea where she was going.

"What is wrong with this place?!" she shouted.

When the echoes faded, she moved her hands off her ears so she could pump her arms as she ran.

That's when she got her answer.

"It's a weapons testing area."

The voice in her ear was unmistakable, and she was so shocked she screamed.

"PETEY!"

She reached up to her shoulder and grabbed him, then hugged him to her cheek.

"Aw, come on!" he complained. "You're squishing my Pop-Tart."

He was right. He held a large corner of toaster pastry in his hand, but most of it was crumbling away. He took another bite anyway. "It's good, but I like the ones with frosting better."

"How did you get that?" Gabby asked. "Were you in

my bag? How did you get in my bag? Where are Sharli and Sneakers? What—"

Her next question was cut off when a wide circle of orange hit the ground next to them. Instantly, the red dirt disappeared, replaced by bubbling tar. Gabby screamed, pinwheeled her arms, and dove forward, arms outstretched, holding Petey so they wouldn't fall in.

"What just happened?!" Gabby wailed.

"So cool," Petey said, taking another bite of Pop-Tart. "Weapons on Mars do *everything*. We should probably take cover, though."

"You think?!"

Gabby scrambled to her feet and ran from the bubbling tar pit, then looked around. The nearest place to hide was a group of boulders: five or six giant, bulbous stones stuck together like a tower of chewed-up gum. She dove behind them, just as a loud hum filled the air, and the ground where she'd just been standing collapsed in on itself. She climbed the rock closest to her and looked down at the wreckage. The ground had become a bottomless pit.

"Mega-low-frequency implosion!" Petey cheered. "Awesome!"

"No!" Gabby shot back. "Not awesome. This place is horrible. Are Sneakers and Sharli here?"

"Not here-here, but yeah, on Mars. They're with the Martians," Petey replied. "The other kinds of Martians. The real ones—the ones who gave the Earth-Mars its name."

"I don't care which Martians," Gabby said. "They're the Martians who have Sneakers and Sharli, on a planet that's a war zone!"

"Okay, time out," Petey said. "Mars is *not* a war zone. It's, like, the most advanced planet ever. They make the most cutting-edge weapons in the universe. It's awesome!"

Another explosion sounded and the ground shook.

Petey pumped his fist. "Yes!"

Gabby couldn't believe it. She put him on an outcropping of the rock so she could look him in the eye.

"Petey, this isn't awesome," she said gently. "I guarantee these explosions are hurting a lot of Martians."

Petey made a buzzing noise like she'd gotten an answer wrong on a quiz show. "Martians *aren't* getting hurt," he said. "I told you, this is a testing area. No one's supposed to be here, so no one's getting hurt."

"If no one's supposed to be here, how come there was a Holographic Acclimation Booth?!"

"A *Mobile* Holographic Acclimation Booth. The mobile ones pop up wherever they're needed. And it's like the Martian said—you rode the tail end of the purple portal wave, so your aim was off. You ended up here, so a mobile booth showed up to catch you. Now the *stationary* booths are different—"

Petey's voice cut off as the rock formation he stood on glowed bright yellow, then vanished. Petey plummeted. Gabby dropped to her knees and caught him a second before he hit the ground.

"Are you okay?" she asked.

He grinned. "Disintegrator Ray! *Mega* awesome!"

"*Not* mega awesome!" Gabby insisted. "We have to get out of here or we will get seriously hurt!"

Petey looked up at her, and for the first time it seemed to sink in that they weren't just checking out a testing area, they were actually in the line of fire.

"Oh yeah," he said, nowhere near as bothered as Gabby thought he should be. "We should go, then." He hopped onto her jacket and shimmied up until he was back on her shoulder. "Run that way. I'll tell you when to turn."

Gabby didn't stop to question. She ran. Then she asked between panting breaths, "How do you know the way out?"

"Coolest school field trip ever," he said. "Plus, I have the Mars VR Tour. My friends from home and I use it to hang out on Mars all the time. I'll show it to you when we get back."

Gabby didn't even want to think about going back

128

until she had Sharli and Sneakers. Once she did, she was pretty sure she wouldn't want to go anywhere near Mars again—*either* Mars—even in virtual reality.

"To the left," Petey said. "That shimmery spot on the big rock—the one that looks like a plarquoot."

Gabby had no idea what a plarquoot was, but given that the rock was at least forty feet tall and looked like a hulking beast with spikes all over its body, Gabby hoped she never met one in real life. The only part of the rock that wasn't terrifying was the shimmering area on what Gabby imagined would be the plarquoot's leg. It was a smaller area than the shimmering portal she walked through to get out of the Mobile Holographic Acclimation Booth—it only came up to her knees—but it still looked the same. Gabby felt certain Petey was right and it would lead them out of this place.

"Whooo!" Petey crowed. "Faster, Gabby!"

Gabby was running as fast as she could, but she managed to find one last gear. The hot air rasped in her throat and her legs ached.

She was almost there. Just a little farther.

Then a high whine rang through the air and the ground under Gabby turned to ice. She slammed down and slid on her stomach.

She couldn't feel Petey on her shoulder anymore. "Petey?!" she cried. "Are you there?"

Gabby felt tugging on her curls as Petey settled onto the back of her neck. "Freeze-O-Later ray! Aweeeeesssooooome!"

He was still whooping when Gabby slid into the shimmery spot on the plarquoot-shaped rock. She squeezed her eyes closed, afraid of what she might find on the other side.

chapter
TWELVE

Gabby kept sliding. Was there ice on the other side of the portal, too?

She opened her eyes and saw she was belly-down on burgundy-colored marble tiles. Then she lifted her head and came face-to-face with what she could only describe as a giant cockroach. Gabby shuddered, and the cockroach gave her the stink eye before it harrumphed and walked away.

That's when Gabby noticed it was wearing a business suit.

"So what do we do now?" Petey said. He had slid off the back of Gabby's neck and now stood in front of her face.

He reached out for one of her curls, pulled it, and let it go. "Boi-oi-oi-oi-oing!"

Gabby quickly sat up and shrugged off her knapsack. She opened it and nodded inside. "You should get in and hide," she said softly.

Petey laughed out loud. "Why? Look around."

Gabby looked.

It seemed like she was in a very tall, very posh lobby. Couches, plush chairs, and other oddly shaped upholstered items lined the walls, but not only on the floor. The seating stretched up as high as Gabby could see, with all kinds of winged or otherwise airborne creatures zipping around before resting on them. Petey was right; he was far from unusual here. Gabby had been an alien babysitter for almost a year now; she'd thought she'd seen a lot, but the breadth of species in front of her was impossible to fully take in. Sure, she saw large slug-creatures, and blobs of ooze . . . those were normal to her by now. But she also saw an almost-featureless stone slab the size of a glacier munching on what looked like an alien hamburger, a bat-like creature with a zombie head and a spiked tail, and then something she thought was a neon-yellow fuzzy beanbag sprouted two large furry hands and used them to walk out of the room. Even the humanoid creatures had different numbers of limbs, heads, and facial features from what Gabby was used to, and in configurations she'd never imagined outside a post-horror-movie-marathon fever dream.

"We really are on another planet, aren't we?" Gabby said. She watched a headless man whose six-eyed face was on his chest play some kind of card game with what looked like a sentient sweater. "Are they all Martians?"

"Here?" Petey said. "None of 'em. This is a visitor center. Tourists hang out here if they just want a break or if they're waiting for a guide or something. Like there—look!"

Petey pointed, and Gabby saw a sleek silver metallic humanoid with black pin-striping stride into the area. Much like the robot Gabby met in the Mobile Holographic Acclimation Pod, this one looked like steel but moved with flowing grace. *Unlike* the one from the Mobile Holographic Acclimation Pod, this one didn't have a metallic skull head. Its metallic head was shaped like a blooming flower. "Tour group from Glarbellia Five, this way!" she said.

At least, Gabby thought the female voice came from the robot—its flowery visage didn't move in the slightest.

As a group of giant furry squid-creatures scurried toward the flower-faced woman, Gabby turned back to Petey. "Are all Martians robots?"

Petey squinched his face like she'd just emanated a nasty odor. "They're not *robots*. They have wearable tech suits. Totally customized, with climate control, water filtration systems, Multi-Meganet access . . . and you can trick 'em out with anything, like ultra-speed, or blaster repellent, or a jet pack and wings. I totally asked Micro Claus to give me one last year, but I only got their VR sales kit, and a note in my stocking that said the cheapest one cost the same as the combined GDP of all the planets in the Thraxion Solar System. But I also got an RC drone, so that was cool."

Gabby had questions, but she didn't ask them because suddenly everything around her disappeared. Instead she saw a building—a tall, thin tower that looked like it was made of red mercury. Its metal seemed to move and slide around, even though the tower never changed shape. It rose high into the sky in one skinny line, except for three bulbous donuts, each one a darker shade of red than the one beneath it. At the top of the tower sat the biggest donut of all—a huge, bright red umbrella-saucer, far wider than anything beneath it.

As quickly as it came, the image disappeared.

Gabby snatched Petey up in her hands. "I know where Sneakers is! He showed me!"

She described exactly what she'd seen, and Petey nodded. "Sure, I know where that is. It's in Plenopsis. It's on the other side of the planet."

Gabby's jaw dropped. "The other side of the *planet*?

Please tell me Mars is really, really small compared to Earth."

"I'll tell you that if you want, but it's not true." Then he grinned. "Wanna know how big Mars is?"

"How big?"

"Four times the size of Earth." Petey grinned wider. "That's the same size as Uranus."

Petey managed to keep a straight face for exactly two seconds after that. Then he laughed so hard he fell on the floor. Despite their situation, watching him was so funny that Gabby had to bite her cheeks to keep from joining in.

"Petey—"

"Get it?!"

"I get it," Gabby assured him, "but if Mars is that big, how do we get to Plenopsis? Won't it take days?"

Petey was still laughing, though it started to subside. "You mean because the planet's as big as—"

"I get it!" Gabby said. "But seriously, how do we get to Sneakers and Sharli?"

Petey sat up and caught his breath. "Easy," he said. "Aeroway system. We'll be there in no time. Come on."

He walked out like he owned the planet. Gabby quickly got up, shrugged on her purple knapsack, and followed him. He wasn't the only tiny being in the Visitor Center, and Gabby had to watch her feet to make sure she didn't step on or bump into anyone else, like the group of guinea pig creatures who stood on their back legs and all wore matching shirts as if they might have been a school group. Gabby got so distracted watching them that she smacked right into someone who resembled a walking pine tree. The tree was exactly Gabby's height, and it took them so long to do that dance where they kept stepping into each other's path that she almost lost sight of Petey. She found him just as he was leaving the Visitor Center, and she ran out after him.

Gabby blinked and shielded her eyes. It was bright out, and when she gazed up, she understood why. The sun took up most of the sky. Yet while this sun was much bigger and brighter than Earth's, it seemed cooler. Her face tingled in the chill, and she was glad she had her purple puffer jacket.

The Visitor Center had emptied onto a city street, and while it was very different from any city street Gabby had ever experienced, it was just familiar enough for her to recognize. Buildings rose on either side, pedestrians clogged the walkways, and countless video billboards hawked all kinds of products.

There were still differences, though. Unlike on Earth, the giant video billboards weren't mounted on anything; they floated in midair. Also unlike on Earth, everything in this city was built not only for those who traveled on foot—or paw, or wheel, or oozy pseudopod—but also those who flew, or floated, or otherwise got around through the air. Buildings had what looked like main entrances with awnings and fancy doorways on several levels, and while she and Petey walked, scores of creatures flew above them. It seemed like they traveled in well-organized tiers, even though Gabby couldn't tell what separated one row from another.

While those in the air had the benefit of flight, it also looked like they had less space in which to maneuver. They stayed reasonably close to the buildings, as if they were on sidewalks, to avoid a constant stream of what had to be vehicles—blurs that whizzed through the air so quickly that Gabby saw them only as a wild skein of contrail streaks in red, blue, or orange. Unlike planes or cars on Earth, these made no sound at all. If Gabby didn't see them, she wouldn't even know they were there. They zipped through without ever stopping for cross-traffic; flyers who wanted to cross the air-street went to a higher altitude. Gabby could see them against the sky like a layer of tiny gnats.

Since all the vehicles zipped through the sky, the actual street was wide open and probably would have been pleasant to walk around if it wasn't so crammed with bodies. Petey was tiny and could zip between other creatures' legs. Gabby had to dodge and dart to keep up, which wasn't easy when she had to keep her eyes locked on Petey so she wouldn't lose him. That was probably for the best; it stopped her from getting distracted by the wide variety of aliens in her path.

What remained distracting were the mini-drones—little screens the size of a hand-held tablet computer that whizzed through the air and kept pace with different pedestrians, showing them commercials. Thanks to the universal translator the Martian had painted on the back of her neck, Gabby understood the drone nearest to her and could tell the ads were directed specifically toward her. "Earthling" came up frequently, as did "visiting" and the phrase "not *that* Mars." Something was definitely lost in translation, though, since she was fairly sure "pimple trampoline stew" was nothing she'd ever want.

Petey slipped into another school group—this one consisting of fire hydrant–sized walking balls of ragmop-fur, the tallest one carrying a sign that read FOLLOW ME—but he never came out the other side. Gabby's heart sped up and her skin prickled. Had she lost him? She spun around but saw only the wild, unfamiliar sights of this new planet. It was dizzying. She unzipped her jacket and grabbed her dad's dog tags through her shirt. She needed the pressure of their hard edges pushing into her skin to keep her from passing out.

For the first time ever in her life, she felt completely lost and alone.

Is this what it was like for the aliens she babysat on Earth?

"Hah!" Petey cried as he landed on top of Gabby's mini-drone. "You are *slow!*"

"Petey!" Gabby almost sobbed with relief. "I thought I'd lost you. Please stay close, okay? Don't run off."

Petey leaped off the mini-drone and onto Gabby's sleeve. He shimmied back up to her shoulder. "Why would I run off? We're here. We're in the Aeroway loading dock. Look down."

Gabby did and saw she was standing just inside the edge of a thick red rectangle painted on the ground. The rectangle was about the size of a small moving van, and crowded with other humanoids, walking carpets, and other extras from the *Star Wars* cantina scene. Above them, flying creatures hovered at different levels in the same rectangular area.

Then a long shadow slid into the sky above them all. As Gabby stared at it, curious, a rectangle about the size of the one on which Gabby was standing glowed bright red, and the red beam extended down, covering first the flying creatures, and then everyone in the rectangle on the ground in that same glow. The light felt hot on her skin, and the heat quickly intensified until she was sure she might burst into flames . . .

. . . and the next thing she knew she was sitting on an

orange molded plastic bench, facing another bench just like it. All the creatures who had been with her in the rectangle of light sat on the benches as well, and they all seemed perfectly comfortable, lost in their own thoughts as they gazed into space, pulled out an electronic device, or—in the case of a six-legged mauve ogre-like creature—clipped their nails. She even saw one decidedly human-looking passenger pull out a *New York Times*.

Gabby heard something squeak and looked up. Petey must have climbed onto her head and jumped, because he was now sitting in one of the many hand straps that hung from a metal pole running around the perimeter of the moving vehicle. He pumped his legs and moved the hand strap like a swing.

"Are we in a subway?" Gabby asked.

"Aeroway," Petey said, nodding to the opposite window, through which Gabby could indeed see they were up in the air, "but yeah, same idea. Except we're moving fast enough to go all the way around the planet in an hour."

Across the car, the human with the newspaper suddenly glowed bright red and disappeared. Gabby jumped and yelped out loud. Several passengers gave her dirty looks before they settled back into what they were doing. Petey took a flying leap off the swing and landed on her head, then grabbed a curl and dove forward, dangling upside down in front of her face.

"Wow, freak out much?" he asked.

"Ow!" Gabby said, wincing. "Okay, you really need to stop that. And I'm not freaking out for no reason. That guy just disappeared!"

Yet even as she said it, four other creatures from around the car also glowed bright red and disappeared, while a whole cluster of new creatures popped into the car in a similar burst of color. Gabby realized what must be happening before Petey even explained it.

"That's how you get on and off the Aeroway," he said. "Catch!"

He somersaulted off her curls, and Gabby caught him in her cupped hands.

"Grab me a Pop-Tart?" he asked. "We've got a little while before our stop."

"Sure." Gabby pulled off her knapsack and rummaged around. She opened the wrong napkin first and found the fish sticks, then closed that up and found the other napkin, with the Pop-Tarts inside. She pulled them out, and her stomach roared so loudly, a bunch of aliens gave her the stink-eye. She offered an apologetic smile, then broke a Pop-Tart and gave half to Petey. He had to spread his arms wide to grab it, then balance the bottom on Gabby's jeans while he stood to nibble at it.

Gabby munched on her own half. She pretended to

give it her full attention so it wouldn't be obvious she was checking out the other Aeroway riders as they blinked in and out of view. There were a near-endless variety of aliens, including several Martians in their sleek robotic suits. The more of these she saw, the more Gabby realized that Petey was right, the suits were indeed customized. They all looked fairly humanoid, but not only did each one have its own unique head shape, but also its own body shape. Some were long and sleek, others looked stockier, with streamlined lumps and bumps that Gabby imagined held some of the plussed-out options Petey had mentioned.

She thought she was being very subtle in her Martian inspection. Then a nearby Martian holding a grip-strap frowned and pointed a finger at her. Gabby blushed and was about to apologize, but before she could, the Martian's fingertip glowed ice blue and Gabby's Pop-Tart vaporized.

"You prob'ly don't want to make the Martians mad," Petey said. Then he took an exaggeratedly huge bite of his own Pop-Tart half. "Mmmm! This is *so good*! Bummer you don't have one anymore."

With a flick of her finger, Gabby snapped the rest of his Pop-Tart out of his hands, then caught it and took her own huge bite.

"Aw, come on!" he complained.

"I'll get you another, but first you have to tell me ..." Gabby lowered her voice in case anyone was listening in. "When did you get into my knapsack? How did you get away when Sneakers and Sharli were taken?"

"Easy," he said. "I was in Sneakers's vest pocket, and I jumped into the grass when they activated their portal. Then I jumped on you when I saw you going in."

Gabby was impressed. "'Cause you wanted to help me save them. That's pretty admirable, Petey."

Petey blushed, then he rolled his eyes and shrugged. "Nah. I just didn't wanna miss out if they were going some-place cool. And see? Turns out they were!"

Gabby hid her smile. She knew she had it right the first time. She reached into her knapsack and pulled out the last Pop-Tart, which she happily handed to Petey. He balanced it on her lap and grinned—the full Pop-Tart was even taller than him.

"If this was frosted, this would be the happiest day of my life."

He dug in, while Gabby kept her eyes pointedly focused on nothing so she wouldn't anger any more laser-beam-happy Martians.

That's when reality hit her and she broke out in goose bumps.

She was *on another planet.*

She was on *Mars*—and not *that* Mars. She was who-knew-where but at least a gajillion miles from home, with no idea how she'd ever get back. How had the little purple circle even gotten her here? How was she even breathing? And what about all those sci-fi movies where an astronaut goes way out into deep space, but then time moves differently super-far away, and when the astronaut comes back after what seemed like a day, a hundred Earth years have passed? Would that happen to her? Would she go home and find out everyone she had ever known was super-old or dead? Would she come back younger than her great-great-granddaughter?

Then she gasped as she thought of the most pressing question of all.

"Petey," she asked, "that translation stripe the Martian painted on my neck—will that stay on forever? 'Cause an A in French would be awesome."

Petey didn't answer. Gabby looked down at him. He had dropped the Pop-Tart and was staring straight ahead, frozen.

He looked scared.

"Petey?"

Petey gestured for her to lean closer. Gabby bent down low so her ear was near his head.

"I might have forgotten that Plenopolis is a restricted area," he said. "Martians only. I don't think anyone likes that we're here."

Gabby had been trying to avoid looking at the other passengers, but now she picked up her head and gazed around. Every other kind of alien had disappeared from the Aeroway car. Only metal-clad Martians remained—seven of them—and none of these had fanciful, flowered faces. All their heads were combinations of sharp edges, laser eyes, and serrated protuberances . . . all of which were pointed directly at Gabby and Petey.

"State your business," came a female voice.

Gabby had no idea which Martian was speaking, but she didn't sound happy.

"Stall them," Petey whispered. Then he grabbed one of her curls and swung over her shoulder, out of sight. The hair-swinging hurt, but Gabby didn't even wince. She had to trust that Petey knew what he was doing. Instead she smiled at the Martians.

"Hi! Hey!" she said brightly. Then she spoke to the silver Martian directly in front of her. "Wow, you are *really* shiny. I can totally see my reflection in you! Do you use a special polish or something? Because my bike could seriously use a shine like this."

A large needle unfolded from the robot's torso and pointed at Gabby's eyes.

"Your business," it said in a deep male voice. "Who gave you permission to access Plenopolis?"

Gabby's brain tap-danced, and she hoped the Martians couldn't hear her heart thudding. "Okay, well, um, those are really two different questions. My business is babysitting, and I'm pretty good at it, I have to say. I mean, not so much today, I guess, but usually I'm really—"

There was a loud whirr as the other six robots unfolded sharp, pointy objects from their torsos.

"We need the name of the Martian who gave you permission to enter Plenopolis," the female voice said. "You have five seconds. Five . . . Four . . ."

Gabby's stomach twisted. Should she make up a name? What would they do if she got it wrong?

"Three . . . Two . . ."

"Petey?" Gabby squeaked.

She didn't mean it as an answer; she was hoping he'd tell her what to do. But lights flashed on the face of the Martian in front of her.

"'Petey' is not a legitimate source for access. *Now.*"

All seven sharp objects shot out of the robots' torsos. At the same instant, Gabby's body sizzled all over and her legs glowed bright red. She had exactly enough time to grab her knapsack before she disappeared . . . and all seven knives, bayonets, and needles impaled themselves into the molded orange bench.

chapter
THIRTEEN

"Get down!" Petey shouted in Gabby's ear.

Gabby didn't even realize she was standing. Her heart was still racing triple-time, and she had no idea where she was or what she was doing.

She instantly dropped to the ground and felt the itchy softness of tall red grass all around her. The blades rose higher than Petey, and he had to stomp and make wide sweeping gestures with his arms to move them out of his way so he could stand in front of her.

"What happened?" Gabby asked.

"I pressed the button for an emergency Aeroway stop,"

Petey said. "It just took me a while 'cause I didn't want the Martians to see and stop me."

"They didn't seem happy that we were here," Gabby said. "You said it's a restricted area?"

"Yeah, but we should be okay now," Petey said. "The only bad thing would be if the Martians on the Aeroway got in touch with the ones down here. Then it'd be bad."

Just then, a loud whooping siren filled the air, and Gabby heard the thrum of countless metal footsteps.

"Okay, it's bad," Petey said.

Gabby peeked over the tall grass. She and Petey were at the top of a large hill that looked down on what appeared to be a sprawling park dotted with fountains and statues and crisscrossed by red-pebbled paths. It would have looked beautiful, except the far end of the park was clogged with a sea of metal-suited Martians, weapons bared, marching double-time onto the paths and spreading out in twos and threes.

Gabby ducked back down into the grass. "Please tell me they're not here for us."

"I can," Petey said, "but my mom and dad probably wouldn't be psyched about me lying to the babysitter. There's good news, too, though."

"The Martians' weapons are fake and won't actually hurt us?" Gabby suggested.

"Nah, they'd obliterate us on contact. But look—is that the tower Sneakers showed you?"

Gabby peeked up again. This time she looked beyond the Martian soldiers to what was across from the park. There rose an endless array of identical towers, each of which was tall and thin, made of red metal that seemed to move like mercury. Every tower had three bulbous donuts blooming out of it, each one redder and wider than the one beneath it, and a huge, bright red umbrella-saucer at the very top.

"Yes," Gabby said uneasily. "They *all* look like Sneakers's tower. How will we know which one's right? And how will we get there with all the Martians in the park?"

"I'm the kid, remember? You're supposed to be the one in charge."

"Yeah, but I've never been to Mars—*any* Mars," Gabby countered. "You had that field trip and your virtual reality game."

"Virtual reality *tour*. There wasn't a game level where I had to escape from Martians out to kill me." Then he smiled, nodding. "But when we get back, I'm totally sending an email to the company, 'cause that's a seriously cool idea."

Gabby rested her elbows on the ground and gripped her curls with her hands. "There has to be a way through this. There *has* to be."

She peeked back up through the grass. The park was

big, and all the Martians coming after them had split into small groups, but they were everywhere. Was there any path she and Petey could follow that would keep them out of the Martians' way? It didn't seem like it. Pairs and trios of Martians marched by every scraggly shrub, every statue, every large rock . . .

Gabby stopped scanning and stared at one of the large rocks in the distance. It was red, a darker shade than the grass, and it caught her eye as three Martians in black-and-gray metallic suits tromped past it. Maybe it was the dark metal that made the rock's anomaly jump out to Gabby, but now that she'd noticed it, she couldn't take her eyes off it.

The rock had a blotch of radiant, Day-Glo pink along its bottom left side.

"Do you see that glowy thing?" Gabby whispered to Petey.

"What glowy thing?" he asked.

Gabby was about to answer, when another glint of hot pink caught her eye. She gazed more broadly over the park and realized there were *several* blotches—small splashes of shocking-pink glow spread out across the vista and standing out against the red grass, red rocks, and red statues.

"There's a *bunch* of glowing splotches," Gabby mused. "What do you think they are?"

"I don't know what you're talking about."

"Look," Gabby said. "There's one right at the bottom of the hill."

She took Petey in her hands and held him in front of her face, aiming him so he could peek through the same patch of grass as her and see the same thing she did: a large red rock, right at the nexus of two footpaths at the bottom of the hill. It had been splashed with the bright pink liquid, and the watery blotch radiated a shocking neon glow.

"*That* glowy thing," Gabby whispered. "You see it, right?"

"What, the dog pee?" Petey asked, incredulous.

"No," Gabby said. "I mean the glowing stuff."

"Yeah," Petey said, and the "duh" was clearly implied. "The dog pee."

"No," Gabby insisted. "How many dogs pee neon hot pink?"

Then she gasped and got chills from head to toe because she was sure she knew the answer.

"Up the hill!" A female voice barked the order. Gabby crawled to her right and peered through the grass to see three Martians start tromping toward her and Petey. The hill was steep, but it didn't seem to slow them down. They sped upward, weapons jutting from their armor and ready to strike.

"Grab the back of my jacket and hold on tight," Gabby whispered. "Hurry!"

She lay flat on her stomach. The second she felt the tug of Petey grasping her jacket collar, she commando-crawled down the hill as fast as she could, moving her arms and legs like a gecko to speed her through the tall grass. The rustling grass thundered in her ears. She hoped it wasn't as loud to the Martians, but she didn't stop to listen. She kept going until she was at the large rock, her nose pressed close to the bright pink splotch.

Gabby sniffed in deep.

"Ew, gross!" Petey wailed. "What are you doing?"

"Shhhh!"

"You hear something?"

The voice was male, and it came from somewhere up ahead of them. Gabby willed herself to lie flatter, and she felt Petey slide between the collar of her jacket and her shirt.

She lay there for an eternity, listening to the swish of tall grass as the Martians walked through it, their footsteps getting dangerously close. Pressed up against the pink blotch on the rock, Gabby's nose filled with an ammonia scent so strong her head spun.

"Nothing here," the male voice finally said. "This way!"

Gabby heard the heavy metallic footsteps stomp off. She let her breath out in a whoosh, but when she breathed in deep to refill her lungs, she had to bury her face in her jacket to stifle a coughing fit.

"The pink stuff is definitely pee," Gabby whisper-choked.

"I know," Petey whispered back. "I told you. And it's gross. You think it smells bad for you? For me that's like a giant wall of pee, and we're right up in it. Ew."

"It's *Sneakers's* pee, though, right? Sneakers pees neon pink!"

"Yes! Sneakers is a dog! That's how dogs pee!"

Gabby didn't bother to explain that while alien dogs like Sneakers might pee neon pink, it was hardly a universal trait. "Petey, Sneakers didn't pee at all when I was with him on Earth, but up on the hill I saw pee splotches all over the park. That can't be a coincidence. Sneakers left us a trail of glowing pink pee. That's how we'll find him and Sharli! The trail will lead us to the right tower!"

Martian footsteps crunched nearby. They had to keep moving. Gabby crawled away from the rock, into deeper grass, then peeked up just enough to see the next closest patch of glowing pink. It was on a scraggly red bush. She waited until all the Martian footsteps faded, then crawled her way there. This time it was Petey who looked for the next splotch. He crawled deep into the scraggly bush and climbed to the top, where he had the best view.

"Patch of grass," he whispered when he made his way back to Gabby's ear. "Diagonally to your right."

They made it a system. Being small, Petey usually had

the best cover to look for each new splotch. He'd locate it and memorize where it was, then climb onto the back of Gabby's neck and guide her there. They even worked it out so they didn't have to speak. Petey steered Gabby like a jockey, pulling on different strands of her hair to change her direction and get her to just the right spot each time. Gabby hated that it was taking them so long. She kept thinking about Sneakers and Sharli, and what might be happening to them while she and Petey snaked their way through the large park. But caution was the only way they'd avoid getting caught, and Sneakers and Sharli would be in even worse shape if she and Petey were blasted to smithereens.

One of the pee-splotches was at the base of a statue—one of the red metal hulks that dotted the park. It was surrounded by a round, red-pebbled clearing that offered no cover, so Gabby stayed in the thick grass while Petey looked for the next trail marker. Left alone, Gabby stared at the statue. It was strange. It looked like a giant, opened jack-in-the-box, but with a massive U-shaped magnet on the spring instead of a clown. There was a large inscription on its pedestal, and thanks to the translator painted on her neck, she could read it clearly.

GRAVITATIONAL PULL DESTABILIZER. SUCCESSFULLY USED TO PULL FERROS OUT OF ORBIT AND PLUNGE IT INTO AN ICE AGE.

As she let the words sink in, Petey hopped onto her neck. He tugged a curl on her right side, but Gabby heard Martian footsteps in exactly that direction, so she didn't want to move just yet. Instead she reached back, pulled Petey off her neck, and brought him next to her head. "That statue," she whispered. "Is it a statue of a *weapon*?"

Petey checked it out, and his eyes danced excitedly. "Yeah!" he whispered back. "I told you Mars makes the coolest weapons ever! And this one's *super* awesome. Mars sold the Gravi-Pull—that's what people who really know about this stuff call it—to some other planet that was at war with Ferros, right? So that other planet put the Gravi-Pull on an outer moon of another planet in Ferros's solar system, and when no one was expecting it . . ."

Petey mimed turning a crank like the one on the jack-in-the-box, then leaped up, arms wide, and whispered, "*BLAM!* Out comes the Magnetorizor, and *BZZZZ*, pulls the *whole planet* out of orbit! The whole thing! How kragphemous is that?!"

"Kragphemous?" Gabby asked.

"You know, cool," Petey said. "Tough. Hard-core. Kragphemous."

"Uh-huh," Gabby said.

She heard Martian voices getting closer, so she put her finger over her lips and waited for them to pass. Then she whispered, "But there were living things on Ferros, right? And if the Gravi-Pull caused an ice age, didn't a lot of the living things die?"

Petey scrunched his eyebrows and tilted his head. He opened his mouth, but then he closed it again, like he didn't know what to say. "I'm not sure," he finally whispered. "I mean . . . I guess."

He looked back up at the Gravi-Pull statue. Gabby could see from his face that it was different for him, somehow . . . but maybe he wasn't sure how.

"Hop back on," she whispered. "The Martians moved. I think we're good to go to the next pee stain."

Petey crawled back onto Gabby's neck and kept guiding her along Sneakers's trail, but every time they neared another statue, Gabby scanned the inscription on the pedestal. Every single statue turned out to be another Martian-created weapon, and the inscription described its greatest triumph.

HARMONIC CONVERGER: CREATED THE EXACT RESONANT TONE TO CRUMBLE THE PLANET ZINK.

ROASTALYZER: RAISED THE TEMPERATURE IN PHLEF FIVE DEGREES IN ONE DAY, MELTING ALL POLAR ICECAPS AND DROWNING EVERY LANDMASS.

MOON ZOOM: PROPELLED ARGRAN'S MOON INTO AN IRREVOCABLE TRAJECTORY TOWARD THE PLANET.

The list went on, and while even Gabby had to admit that

every statue looked like the most ... well ... kragphemous movie prop she'd ever seen, none of the stories were from movies. They were real. Gabby didn't know how many of the destroyed and devastated planets had inhabitants, or how many those inhabitants were able to evacuate and get to other planets, but no matter what, it all seemed pretty awful.

"All the tourists who come here," Gabby whispered to Petey the next time they were far enough away from their hunters, "and everyone who checks out the planet in virtual reality, like you, do they know the Martians destroyed all those planets?"

"It's not like the Martians did it themselves," Petey whispered back defensively. "I mean, they *make* weapons. For other planets. They don't *use* them. I don't even think Mars has been to war. Ever."

"Okay ... but do the tourists know Mars is behind all these wars?"

Gabby could practically hear the eye roll in Petey's voice. "Gabby, they're not. Martians make cool weapons. Cool weapons don't kill planets; species who use cool weapons kill planets."

"With cool weapons they got from Mars," Gabby retorted. "And it's not like the Martians aren't happy about it. Look at all the statues. They're celebrating it."

"Well, yeah!" Petey shot back. Then his voice faded, and

Gabby knew he didn't have a great answer for why. Instead he said petulantly, "Look, if no one wanted the weapons, Mars would make something else. Like . . . I dunno . . . kittens."

Gabby scrunched her brow. "You don't make kittens," she said. "At least, not the way you're thinking."

"They do on Galgathon Five," Petey said. "I'm just saying, whatever happened to all those planets, it's not the Martians' fault."

Gabby would have answered, but the Martians sounded far enough away that she felt like she could move. She commando-crawled to a particularly large boulder, then waited for Petey to climb it and scout out the next splotch.

"Guess what?" he whispered when he hopped back down by her face.

"I'm going to wake up back in bed and this whole day will be a bad dream?"

"That's a terrible guess," Petey said. "If it was all a dream, you'd've never met me."

"Good point. Just tell me, then—what?"

Petey grinned. "We're here."

"Here?"

Gabby warily peeked up from the grass. She hadn't even realized it, but she and Petey had made it all the way across the park. They were right at its edge. The thick grass ended a few feet up ahead, then only a wide, red-pebbled walkway separated them from the first row of towers . . . one of which was marked with a neon-pink pee splotch.

Gabby was so excited she almost forgot to whisper. "That's the one!"

Taking a quick look around, she saw the Martians in their pairs and trios, but at this moment none of them were coming their way.

She looked at the tower; the big pedestrian walkway in front of it was empty in all directions, and the shimmery spot that had to be its entryway, just like all the other Martian entryways she'd seen, called to her like a giant beacon.

Gabby bit her lip, nervous but excited. "I think we can make it."

Petey grinned and hopped onto her shoulder. "Do it!"

Gabby edged to the walkway side of the large rock, using its cover as long as she had it, then sprinted for the pee-marked tower. She tried not to think about the pounding sound of her feet on the pebbles—she just ran for all she was worth, her eyes on the large, shimmery spot. It was a fifty-yard dash away . . . twenty-five . . . ten . . .

Suddenly, a bright red lattice lit up between her and the tower, and Petey yanked her hair so hard she reeled backward.

"OW!" she screamed.

She gasped, but the damage had been done.

"FREEZE!" cried a male voice behind them in the park. "HANDS IN THE AIR AND TURN AROUND! *SLOWLY!*"

Gabby froze, and she felt her blood drain down her body. She didn't want to turn around. She wanted to disappear.

Still, she obeyed. She put up her hands and spun slowly around. The nearest Martian—the one who must have spoken to her—was just across the walkway from her. He had what looked like a small cannon on top of his head, and it was pointed right at her. Two more Martians flanked him, one on either side.

Behind them, the entire swarm of Martians that had been hunting them now poured out of the park, all with their weapons drawn.

Gabby and Petey were cornered.

chapter FOURTEEN

*G*abby blinked back tears as the horde of Martians ran toward them. She wasn't crying because she was terrified, nor because her head still throbbed from Petey yanking her hair. She was crying because she was frustrated. She knew she was the one who'd messed up.

"The red grid lights," she said. She knew Petey could hear her; she could feel him holding on to the back of her neck. "They were lasers, right?"

"Motion-sensor high-intensity laser alarms," Petey said. "Sorry I hurt you. I could've just jumped away, but I didn't want you to get vaporized. I'd be in big trouble with my parents if you did."

Gabby laughed despite herself. "I shouldn't have shouted. We'd be okay if I'd kept quiet."

The first three Martians were right in front of them now, with the rest of them just behind. Gabby knew she only had a couple of seconds.

"Run and hide, Petey," she said urgently. "Don't let them catch you, too. I'll try to get out of this, I swear."

"How?" Petey asked.

Gabby had no idea, and no time to think about it before the Martian with the cannon on his head reached her and roughly pulled her arms behind her back. She felt Petey leap off her neck and hoped he managed to get someplace far away without being seen.

"Let's go," said the Martian holding Gabby's arms. "We're taking you for recycling."

More Martians surrounded her, pressing close so she couldn't escape. She saw nothing but her own warped reflection in their metallic silver, purple, black, and gold suits.

"Recycling?" she asked as they marched her forward.

"Yes," the Martian holding her said. "We'll kill you, but in the process we'll break you down into all your individual cells so we can reuse them for everything from fuel, to plant food, to textiles. We try to keep our executions eco-friendly."

"That's weirdly almost admirable," Gabby said.

As she kept marching forward, Gabby leaned this way and that to see beyond the immediate circle of Martians surrounding her. All she saw was another circle of Martians beyond them, and then another beyond those. There was no possible way out.

She wondered if anyone at home would know she'd been recycled, or if they'd just think she'd been kidnapped, or run away. She imagined her dad hearing the news in Miami. Would he fly back home to comfort Mom and Carmen? Or would he blame Alice for Gabby's disappearance? Gabby could imagine them fighting over it, and then Carmen getting caught up in some kind of angry custody battle.

Gabby also wondered about Edwina. Did she know Gabby was on Mars? *This* Mars? Her step lightened a bit as she imagined Edwina finding out and marshaling all of A.L.I.E.N. to bring back her, Petey, Sharli, and Sneakers. Gabby could even imagine the sound of Edwina's voice ringing out as she swept in at the last second to save her before she was recycled.

Just then a voice *did* ring out . . . but it wasn't Edwina's. The voice was a strong soprano, booming and majestic, and it froze every Martian in their tracks. In unison, they all turned to face the park, tilted back their heads, and raised their arms up in a high V—including the Martian who'd been holding Gabby.

Suddenly, Gabby was free. No one was even looking at her.

Why? What was going on?

Gabby looked around and saw the source of the voice.

It was Petey.

He stood on the head of a burgundy-metal-suited Martian and sang out loud: "*Mars, oh, Mars, we loyal are / Sing your praises near and far / Honor thee and cheer your name / As you spread your fiery flame . . .*"

The song went on, filled with glowing praise for Mars and its superiority in the universe, and the Martians remained completely still. If Gabby didn't know better, she'd be positive they were actual robots, not creatures in metal suits, because it seemed impossible that anyone could hold their arms so perfectly straight in the air for so long without getting terrible cramps.

"Petey?" Gabby asked as she moved closer to him. "What's going on?"

Petey shook his head, but he didn't stop singing. In fact he leaned extra-hard on some of the words and stared at Gabby while he did, as if to make sure she heard them clearly.

"*Let our ANTHEM loudly blare / Spread our pride through*

everywhere / SHOW ALLEGIANCE ABSOLUTE / HEAR THE SONG AND ALL SALUTE!"

Petey let the last note ring out. When it finished, the Martians rumbled back to life—for a second. Then Petey took a deep breath and started in again. "*Mars, oh, Mars we loyal are . . .*"

The Martians immediately snapped back into position.

Gabby grinned. She got it now. Petey was singing the Martian anthem, and Martians clearly took their anthem *very* seriously. As long as he was singing, none of the Martians would move. It was brilliant, except Petey's face was turning red from endlessly belting the song. He couldn't go on forever, and the second he stopped they were doomed all over again.

Unless . . .

Gabby pulled out her cell phone and called up the voice record function. The next time Petey started the anthem, she reached up and held the phone as close to him as she could. When he reached the end, she stopped recording but motioned for him to keep singing—she had some work to do. Petey understood, but his face was even redder now, and his voice was starting to strain on the higher notes. Gabby didn't have much time before it gave out entirely. She quickly shrugged off her backpack and rummaged inside until she found her Bluetooth speaker. It was shaped like an incredibly cute, big-eyed panda bear, with rounded ears on top—the littler kids she babysat loved that. Gabby quickly synced her phone to the speaker, and when Petey finished the anthem once more, Gabby held up a hand to him—*Stop*. He did, and Gabby immediately played back the song from her phone. It rang out through the speaker, even louder than when Petey sang it himself.

It worked. The Martians stayed in position. They didn't budge.

Petey hopped off the Martian's head and slid down his back, where Gabby caught him. "Thanks," he said breathlessly. "I don't think I could have done another round."

"Thank *you*," Gabby said. "You have a really good voice."

Petey rolled his eyes. "Don't tell my mom. She wants me to join the Minisculeans of Earth Youth Group Choir. *Not* interested."

"Deal. Now let's figure out how to get into Sharli and Sneakers's tower."

Gabby set her phone's playback on a continuous loop so the anthem would play over and over, then she and Petey left the Martian horde behind. They ran back to the tower that was splashed with Sneakers's hot-pink pee. She gave the Martians one more glance, just to make sure they weren't watching, but they all steadfastly faced the park.

"They have to face southeast during the anthem," Petey said, guessing her question. "That's the direction of

Grarglebok from Mars; Grarglebok's the first planet to buy any of their weapons."

It wasn't the most poetic reason Gabby could imagine, but at least it kept the Martians from seeing what Gabby and Petey were up to. "Okay," she said. "Let's see how powerful this thing is."

She rummaged for something expendable in her knapsack. There were the metallic foot springs, the cloth napkin full of fish sticks . . . Then Gabby whipped out the other cloth napkin—the one that had held the Pop-Tarts. She zipped her knapsack back up, shrugged it onto her back, then tied the ends of the napkin into a knot so it had some weight. "Here we go," she said, and lobbed the knotted napkin toward the tower.

ZAP! The lattice sprung into view like a lightning bolt, and the napkin vaporized instantly. It didn't even leave any ash.

"Whoa," Petey said. "That was seriously kragphemous."

"Kragphemous . . . and dangerous," Gabby said. "But there has to be a way through."

The Martian anthem restarted, and Gabby inwardly thanked whoever created the continuous repeat option on her phone. Getting through the laser lattice was a puzzle, and she needed time to figure it out.

Slowly, she stepped closer to the building. The lasers snapped to life, and Gabby inspected them while they sizzled. She noticed the lasers came from a series of small, perfectly circular red eyes along the tower. Each eye telescoped just an inch or two out from the building when the lasers activated, and each projected a different section of the mesh. The eye responsible for the section of lasers in front of Gabby was about twenty feet up on the tower.

The mesh itself was like a chain-link fence, far too tight for Gabby to ever squeeze through. She couldn't stick more than the tippy toe of her sneaker in without it hitting a beam and disintegrating.

Petey, however . . .

Gabby thought about his dexterity, how he was always scrambling up her jacket, or swinging and somersaulting off her hair. Even when Sharli had sent him spiraling around her house, he'd been unafraid.

Petey could conceivably get to the door, but Gabby couldn't. Not unless she could disarm the lasers entirely. Or if she were a Martian and had her own suit made of mirrored metal to deflect the laser light rays.

Mirrored metal to deflect the laser light rays.

Gabby's heart thudded. She had an idea. A good idea—one Zee would be proud of—but she couldn't do it without putting Petey into incredible danger. Petey was just a kid and her responsibility. There was no way she could knowingly risk his life.

Except there was another kid and an alien dog, and they were her responsibility, too. And while she'd never choose any of them over the others, she also couldn't live with herself if she left this place without trying everything she could to rescue Sharli and Sneakers.

Gabby took Petey off her shoulder and looked him in the eye. "The holes in the laser mesh," Gabby said. "You think you could fit through them?"

Petey turned to look at the glowing red lattice. Each hole was about half his height, and while its width was thinner than Petey if he stood with his arms and legs spread wide, Gabby knew he *could* fit through if he got a running start and dove, with his hands over his head and his legs together.

She wasn't interested in the physics of it though. She wanted to know how he felt about his chances.

When Petey turned back to her he was grinning.

"Easy."

Gabby relaxed the teeniest bit, but Petey was just getting started.

"Wait'll you see it," he said. "This is gonna be the sweetest recue ever. I dive through the laser fence, run through the door, then I zoom around like a mini-ninja until I find Sneakers and Sharli, and then—"

"Whoa, whoa, whoa," Gabby said. "You're not going in by yourself."

"Uh . . . yeah I am. Unless you've got a Shrink-O-Zapper in that backpack." Then his eyes lit up. "*Do* you?"

He looked so excited, Gabby almost wished she did. "No. But I don't need it. I have a better idea."

She reached deep into the pocket of her purple puffer jacket and pulled out the small rectangular lip gloss compact Madison had given her earlier that day. She knelt down and took very careful aim, then slipped it gently through a low hole in the mesh.

"What's that?" Petey asked.

"You'll see. First I need you to try something."

Gabby reached down to the bottom of her knapsack, grinning as she again pushed past Zee's springing shoe covers—Gabby couldn't wait to thank Zee for the inspiration—and pulled out a pair of ballpoint pens, the kind with the clicker at the top to retract the tip. She twisted each pen apart, then pulled out the ink tubes. Each one had a small spring at the end, which she quickly yanked off.

"Sit, please," she told Petey. "Legs out in front of you."

He did as he was told. Gabby bent out the ends of the

springs, then re-bent them around Petey's sneakers. Petey brightened as he realized what Gabby was trying to do.

"Best. Sitter. Ever," he said.

Gabby laughed. "Not sure your mom would agree. Let's try 'em out."

She held out a finger, and Petey grabbed it to pull himself up. Thanks to Gabby's handiwork, the spring-tops were now securely fastened over his sneakers, while the springs themselves rested perfectly in the middle of his feet. He took a few test bounces, then within seconds he was bouncing for all he was worth, rising to eye level with Gabby.

"This is so cool!" he shouted.

"Shhh!" Gabby reminded him. It was great the Martians were fully engrossed in the anthem, but they were still nearby, and she'd rather they didn't overhear Gabby and Petey and figure out exactly where they were. Gabby grabbed the Minisculean at the apex of his next jump, then explained what she needed him to do. "I won't lie," she said when she finished. "It's very dangerous. If you don't feel comfortable, if you have any worries at all, you don't have to—"

"I'm not worried!" he insisted. "And I don't care about danger. My middle name is Danger."

"No it isn't."

"Sure it is! It's Arkrapharaggog. In my language? 'Danger.'"

Gabby rolled her eyes. She took a deep breath, then set him down on the ground. "Okay, Danger," she said. "Go for it. But be careful."

Petey gave her a cocky point-and-wink. Then he took a few steps back, while Gabby moved just close enough to the tower to blink the red laser lattice to life. Gabby wanted to say something encouraging to Petey, but she didn't want to distract him. If she threw off his rhythm even the slightest bit . . . She didn't even want to think about what would happen.

Petey looked at the lattice, measuring it with his gaze. He set his jaw, narrowed his eyes, then took two loping leaps . . . and dove forward, his arms extended over his head and his legs pointed long. Gabby ached to reach out and yank him away from peril, but instead she gripped her hair in one fist and chewed on her other hand's nails as Petey arced through space . . . and right through the center of a mesh hole. He somersaulted onto the red pebbles on the other side, then stood up with his arms held high, as if he'd just finished an Olympic gymnastics routine . . . or as if he were a Martian listening to his planet's anthem.

Gabby let out her breath in a whoosh. "Great job, Petey. The rest'll be easy."

The rest wouldn't be easy at all, but she thought maybe if she said it out loud, she'd believe it.

Petey didn't seem worried. He strode to the lip gloss compact Gabby had slipped through the mesh. It was almost as long as Petey was tall; he had to squat to pick it up. When he rose with it wrapped in his arms, it reminded Gabby of Ralph Gilland, a fellow Brensville Middle School Orchestra member, holding his standing bass. Ralph could do it, but barely, and the entire operation always looked precarious and unwieldy.

Gabby realized she should have had Petey try holding the lip gloss *before* she put it through the mesh. Now it was too late. She bit her tongue to stop herself from scrapping the mission. Petey believed he could do this; she had to believe in him.

Gripping the lip gloss compact, he bounced into the air. At first he wobbled, and Gabby had a horrible image of him bouncing off course and right into the laser mesh that blazed just a couple feet in front of him, but soon he got used to the extra weight, and bounced straight and true. With each bounce he rose higher . . . then higher still . . . then even higher. . . .

After an eternity he landed on the small telescoping stem of the laser beam projector, around twenty feet in the air. Gabby vaguely heard a triumphant holler. He was so high up she couldn't see exactly what he was doing, but she knew the plan. He had to open the compact, then hold the lip gloss side and dangle the mirror directly in front of the laser eye so its beams would reflect back at itself. If he did it and it worked . . .

The laser mesh snapped out of sight. Gabby grabbed her knapsack and raced forward a split second before she heard Petey squeal, "Hot-hot-hot-*hot*!"

Instantly, the compact fell and the mesh snapped back into place . . . but now with Gabby on the inside.

A moment later, Petey soared down, bounced off the ground, and somersaulted up and into Gabby's outstretched hand.

"Good thing you're fast," he said. "That thing got hot. I could only hold it for a second."

"Did your hands get burned?" Gabby asked.

Petey shook his head and held them out. His fingers looked a little red but not angrily so, and there were no blisters.

"You're good," Gabby said. "But if they hurt, let me know, okay? I have cream in my knapsack."

Petey nodded. He wasn't usually at a loss for words. She wondered if it was just now sinking in, the danger of what he'd accomplished.

"You're really brave," Gabby told him. "I'm proud to be your friend, Petey."

One corner of Petey's mouth turned up. The beginning of a smile.

"Call me Danger," he said.

Gabby smiled back. "Okay, Danger, let's see what's inside."

With no idea what awaited them, Gabby took a deep breath and strode through the wall.

chapter

FIFTEEN

nside the tower, Gabby didn't see much of anything. The room was basically an empty steel-gray cylinder.

She didn't *see* much of anything, but she *heard* a lot.

From outside the tower walls came a flurry of loud, angry voices.

"Where did she go?"

"Where is she?"

"We lost her!"

A roar of rage rang out from the crowd, then Gabby heard the thunder of metallic footsteps grow louder as the horde of Martians they'd evaded outside ran toward the tower.

Apparently, the Bluetooth connection between Gabby's phone and the speaker wasn't strong enough to go through the tower walls. With the anthem no longer playing, the Martians were back on the warpath.

"What if they find us?" Petey asked.

Gabby put a finger to her lips. She didn't think they could hear her through the walls—certainly not over the sound of their own pounding feet—but she didn't want to risk it. If she'd dared to speak, she'd have told Petey she thought they were safe. The Martians had only noticed Gabby in the first place after she'd backed away from the tower—they wouldn't know she'd been trying to get into this particular building. They'd also walked her a good distance away, and they'd been facing the park the entire time Gabby and Petey had worked their way inside.

She *thought* they were safe, but she didn't *feel* safe until the pounding footsteps reached their crescendo, then faded away into the distance.

"We're good. At least for now," Gabby said. Then she looked around the room. "What do you think this place is?"

The cylindrical room they were in was small, maybe the size of one of the food stands back at the fair. When Gabby tilted her head up, she saw the room stretched high above, eventually ending in a steel-gray ceiling. In the very center of the room sat a second cylinder, but this one had an oval cut out of it, like an entryway.

Gabby thought of how the building looked from the outside—skinny with the three wide donuts leading up to the giant dome at the top.

"I bet that's an elevator," she said, looking at the inner cylinder.

"Cool," Petey said. "Where do we take it?"

Gabby had no idea. She'd brought Petey inside, but the elevator gave her no added information. It was blank metal, with only four unmarked buttons to even hint that it did anything at all. She wished Sneakers had marked one of them for her, but she guessed it was harder to get away with peeing inside the building.

Which button should she press? She wished Sneakers could tell her. The dog had been so good about sending Gabby signals when she needed them. She wished there were a way to reach out to Sneakers and tell the dog she desperately needed one now.

Gabby smiled. Maybe there was. Sneakers had already proven he could send images into Gabby's head; maybe he could *receive* images, too.

Gabby stared at the buttons, concentrating on them with

every ounce of energy in her body. In her head she called out to Sneakers, loud as she could. *Which button, Sneakers? How do we get to you? Where are you, Sneakers? Where???*

Minutes ticked by. Gabby started to sweat. She was probably wasting her time. Any second now, someone in the horde of Martians would realize where they'd gone and storm into the tower to grab them for recycling. . . .

Then Gabby saw something, as if it were right in front of her: a view out a window. The view was high in the air, and through it Gabby could see the uppermost dome of another tower.

When the image faded, Gabby slammed her finger into the uppermost button. "They're at the top," she said as the doors slid closed. "When Sneakers looks out the window, he sees the top of the next tower. Hold on tight, Petey."

After everything else Gabby had experienced on Mars, she expected the elevator ride to be equally intense. She thought she and Petey might zip up at hyper-speed, pushed painfully into the floor from G-force pressure.

Instead she felt a lurch as the elevator slowly meandered upward, while tinny Muzak tinkled from an unseen speaker.

"Why am I holding on tight, exactly?" Petey asked.

Gabby had no good answer for that. Elevators,

apparently, were one technological item the Martians hadn't mastered.

A moment later, Petey had another question. "What do we do when the doors open? What if someone's there? My throat's still kinda sore; I don't think I can sing the anthem well enough to help."

"You don't need to," Gabby said. "I have it on my phone, remember?"

She pulled out her phone...which had gone completely black. Gabby's neck hair stood on end. "No ... no—no—no ... it was totally charged!"

"Well, yeah, on Earth!" Petey said. "Batteries drain fast on other planets. Do you have any idea how much power it takes to search for service through space?"

Gabby was only half paying attention. She'd already swung her knapsack in front of her and was rummaging through it for the charger she always kept inside. She couldn't feel it anywhere, so she took the bag all the way off and sat on the elevator floor to dig around.

Suddenly, panic tickled her skin as she remembered.

"No ..." she said, rummaging faster, as if the universe might somehow have changed the past to help her when she needed it most.

"What?" Petey asked.

"I can't recharge the phone. I gave my charger to Carmen back at the fair."

She wheeled to Petey, her eyes desperate. "You need to teach me the song. Now. I'm good with music; I can learn it fast."

"But can you sing? If you're bad, the Martians won't listen."

Gabby didn't have time to answer before the elevator jolted to a stop. In a heartbeat, Gabby grabbed Petey and hid him in her hair, then pressed herself against the wall. It might only give her an extra second if the doors opened on a sea of metal suits, but at least it was something.

The doors did open . . . but Gabby didn't see any Martians, only a rounded metal vestibule. Cautiously, she eased herself and Petey out of the elevator and into a steel-gray circular hall with eight entryways, each of which opened out into another large room—a pie section of the giant dome at the top of the tower, Gabby imagined. She heard the dull sound of footsteps and voices, but they were far away, coming from all the different rooms, and they overlapped into a susurrant murmur too layered for her translator to decipher.

Moving slowly, Gabby tiptoed to the closest entrance. She peered in only long enough to make sure no one was looking her way, then slipped behind the closest thing that could give her cover: a tall metal cylinder, tapered at the bottom. Even with that tapering, the slimmest part was more than wide enough to hide two Gabbys.

Gabby waited a minute, heart thumping, just to be sure no one had seen her. Then she peeked out and saw the cylinder hiding her and Petey was just one of countless similar cylinders—some thinner than Gabby's and some thicker—in a cavernous room teeming with metallic-suited Martians in all shapes and sizes.

"The tubes . . ." Gabby whispered to Petey. "They look kind of like the one in the weapons testing ground. The one I left when I first got here."

"Well, yeah," Petey whispered back. "That's 'cause they *are*. But these are just for Martians. You can tell 'cause they're bigger, and not just on the inside. Martians know all about Mars; they don't need a Holographic Acclimation Booth. So these are just Transport Tubes. They're lower tech, and they come in lots of different sizes: small enough to fit just one Martian, or big enough to fit a bunch of 'em delivering a major weapon . . . unless the weapon's *so* big they have to Shrink-O-Zap it first."

Gabby was impressed. "You know a lot about this stuff," she whispered. "Was this room in your VR tour?"

"I wish! The tour doesn't let you go in the towers. I've got another VR tour that's just about all the weapons and tech from Mars. There's a whole section about the pods. It lets you go in and check 'em out and program 'em ..." He stopped and his eyes got wide. "Can we go in and program one now? I could take you to Minisculea!"

"We have to save Sneakers and Sharli," Gabby said.

"Well, yeah, but like ... after," he said. "You could see my home."

He sounded so sweet and hopeful, Gabby hated to say no. "I think we have to get right back to Earth afterward," she said. "Your parents are probably really worried about all of you."

"Yeah, you're right," Petey said. "I just thought you might want to see it."

"I do," Gabby assured him. "Maybe next time I sit for you. You can get there from Earth, right?"

"Yeah! We have a Minisculean Transport Pod at home! It's—"

Gabby didn't let him finish his sentence. She pulled Petey off her shoulder and put her index finger over his lips so he couldn't speak.

A Martian was coming. The alien's green metal suit was thick, not sleek; it made him look like an armored tank.

Gabby kept Petey's mouth covered and pulled him close, hunching deeper into the shadow between the nearest pod and the wall. From here she couldn't see the Martian, so hopefully it couldn't see her either. She heard the Martian step inside the pod, then heard its door slide closed.

How long did it take for the pod to work? If she ran out of the room right now, would the Martian hear her? Would he suspect anything? Was it even safe to hide behind the pod while it was working? What if it let off radiation, or got burning hot, or—

DING!

The pod chimed pleasantly. Petey peeled her finger off his mouth, then crawled up the front of her jacket to stand back on her shoulder.

"It's done. The Martian's gone," he said, smacking his lips with a grimace. "And your finger tastes like pennies."

"We should get out of here," Gabby said. "I don't think Sharli and Sneakers are in this section."

Gabby leaned out from behind the pod. There were still Martians everywhere, moving in and out of the countless pods in the room. Yet aside from the one they'd just seen, none of them were heading in Gabby and Petey's direction. The flow of traffic actually seemed to move the opposite way, toward the windows at the far end of the dome.

"I don't understand," Gabby whispered to Petey. "If all these Martians are coming to and from the planet through here, why is this part of the room so empty? Why aren't they all coming this way to go down the elevator and back home?"

Petey peered into the room. "'Cause they're all going the other way," he said. "We couldn't see it from down below, but there's a walkway around the edge of the dome—that I *did* see in VR. They probably catch the Aeroway out there, so they'd get dropped off there too. The elevator's gotta be old tech—that's why it was so empty and slow."

Gabby nodded. What Petey said made sense, and it was good for them. If the Martians came in and out of the dome by Aeroway, then the little circular hallway around the elevator was relatively safe. There was no good reason for a Martian to go through there at all, unless maybe someone wanted to go from one dome room to another and was closer to the inside hall than the dome edge. Or maybe if a Martian wanted to go from the dome to one of the lower donut-floors . . . though for all Gabby knew, there was a faster way to do that, too.

This new information made Gabby feel much better about leaving their pod-cover and zipping back into the hall, where there was no cover at all. They might be totally exposed, but they were alone.

"Where do we try next?" Petey asked.

There were still seven more entrances into different parts of the dome. Sharli and Sneakers could be in any of them.

"We just work our way around, I guess," Gabby said.

She stayed close to the wall, which would give her a split second of cover if she heard footsteps coming, and sidled counterclockwise to the next entryway. She dropped to her knees, hoping no one would be looking at the bottom half of the opening, and peered around the edge.

Unlike the first area, this one wasn't one cavernous room. Instead Gabby saw a long hallway with many arched openings, as well as other hallways branching off in different directions. The openings glowed red, and Gabby could see the red laser mesh on the nearest one.

"Prison cells," Petey said, echoing Gabby's own thoughts.

"You think that's where they're holding Sharli and Sneakers?" Gabby asked.

Before Petey could answer, a deep, guttural, raging voice echoed through the circular hallway. "NO, BLINZARRA! THAT'S NOT GOOD ENOUGH!"

Gabby reared back and gasped. "Blinzarra!" she whispered.

"Sharli's mom!" Petey whispered back.

"YOU HAVE TWO MINUTES!" the voice raged again, and this time Gabby heard it clearly come from the entryway directly across from them. The voice was so furious and menacing, every instinct Gabby had told her to run away from it as fast as she could.

But if she did that, she'd never save Sneakers and Sharli.

Gabby tucked Petey into her hair for camouflage, then raced across the hall toward the booming voice.

chapter
SIXTEEN

*g*abby peeked in the doorway, looking for something she could duck behind. Immediately to her left was a red metal statue that looked a lot like the ones she and Petey had seen in the park across from the towers. Gabby didn't bother to look at it closely; she figured it was a safe bet that it commemorated some kind of monstrous weapon that did something equally monstrous to another planet. She was just happy it sat on a large dais. She immediately slipped behind it, then peered over its edge to see what was going on.

She was in some kind of giant, fancy executive office. The curved far wall was all windows that looked out on the same view of the next dome over that Sneakers had shown in his vision. Set back from that was a large desk with several computer screens hovering over it, and a plush wheeled chair that faced the screens and the window. In another area, Gabby saw what had to be a recliner. It was shaped like a large purple hand, with long, fuzzy fingers where someone would stretch out their legs. Gabby saw more chairs around a table set with bowls of food, more scattered statues, a shelving unit filled with all kinds of strange objects that Gabby couldn't place at all, and—

"Gabby!" Petey whispered excitedly in her ear. "Do you see that? That's a rack of Metall-O-Bands. A whole *rack*!"

Gabby didn't know what he was talking about. She did see something right next to the desk that looked like a spinning display unit she'd expect to see holding sunglasses at a drugstore. This one held what looked like watchband-sized strips in all different colors and designs.

"You mean the flat things? What are they?"

"Flat things?" Petey echoed incredulously. "Those are the armor suits! The ones I told you about. A *gajillion* different armor suits!"

He leaped onto Gabby's face, hugging his arms and legs around her cheeks.

"Think he'd miss one?"

Gabby grabbed the back of his shirt and peeled him off her face, but before she could ask him what the little flat strips had to do with high-tech robotic suits, the same booming voice she'd heard from the hallway echoed across the room.

"SO?"

It was coming from somewhere far into the room and off to the right, but Gabby couldn't see the speaker from where she was hidden. She set Petey down and scooted over several feet to the other side of the statue's platform. She peeked over its edge.

Now she saw the other side of the room. It dropped down two steps to an open space with a few scattered chairs, but the most prominent feature was the entire side wall covered with screens. Gabby couldn't count how many there were—they were all different sizes and stretched the entire length and width of the wall. She did notice that most of them showed battle scenes. Gabby glimpsed creatures fighting on the ground in exotic worlds with colored rays like the kind she'd seen in the weapons testing area, and she also saw wide views of outer space, with fleets of ships blasting one another and exploding as they raced among the stars.

She barely had time to take those in, because something else gripped her attention right away. In the very center of the wall sat the largest screen of all. It was as tall as Gabby herself, and so long it would have taken up the entire length of Gabby's kitchen.

On that monitor was Blinzarra, and in a corner of the monitor Gabby saw exactly what Blinzarra was seeing—exactly what Gabby herself could see when she adjusted her position behind the statue platform.

Sharli and Sneakers.

Little three-year-old Sharli was blindfolded. Gabby assumed that was so she wouldn't use her power to move objects with her mind. Sneakers was on a short leash tied down to a hook on the floor. A thick leather muzzle was strapped tightly over his snout.

Standing right behind them was what looked to Gabby like a giant bright pink squid, with at least twenty writhing tentacles. Between his long, oblate head and the tentacles he used as legs, he stood about eight feet tall. Two of his tentacles rested firmly on Sneakers and Sharli, while others undulated in the air. Gabby noticed the angry red suckers on their undersides.

Gabby's blood boiled. She wanted to run and grab Sneakers and Sharli and race out of the room and into the elevator—or better yet into one of the pods to get them off the planet. She wanted to grab something and hurl it at the squid, knocking it out so they'd have time to get away.

But the giant squid wasn't alone.

In a wide arc around him, outside the range of what the squid was showing Blinzarra on the screen, were three Martians. They all wore thickly armored suits, had face masks covered in tiny nozzles, and while they weren't holding any weapons Gabby could see, she felt confident that both the armor and the tubes were ready to shoot out any number of lasers, gases, or other brutal projectiles.

On the large screen, Blinzarra looked ashen. Gabby wasn't surprised. She herself was only Sharli's babysitter, and the sight of the little girl blindfolded, lip quivering as she tried not to cry while she was held captive by a hideous creature, nearly tore her apart. Yet despite Blinzarra's terror, her eyes blazed with fury. When she spoke, her voice was firm.

"You won't get what you want," she said tightly, "but you will get war."

"No, no, no!" came a gruff, offscreen voice. Then the camera angle widened to reveal one end of what looked like a very large conference table, with several different alien species seated around it. The one who had spoken, and who presumably panned the camera wider, was another squid-creature. It looked similar to the one in the room with Gabby, except its skin was slightly redder, and it had a bushy mustache in the middle of its face. It stared right into the lens and raged. "You do *not* represent the planet Esquagon!"

Then he spun to Blinzarra, who was seated right next to him. "He does not represent Esquagon."

Blinzarra stared daggers at the mustached squid. The tendons stood out on her neck. "You say that, but he has my daughter! He took my daughter!"

"And my son!"

A tiny man who looked almost exactly like Petey, except with a goatee, leaped into the shot. He stood on the conference table and moved closer to the camera so he took up the entire frame. "What have you done with Petey, you Esquagonian monster? Where is he? We'll tear up the universe to find him!"

"Awww," Petey said. "You hear that? My dad's gonna tear up the universe to find me."

"We have your son in a separate location," the squid-beast sneered. "He's safe now, but if you don't give me back to Blinzarra, I can't guarantee it will remain the case."

"He's lying," Petey said to Gabby. "He doesn't have me anywhere. I should tell my dad."

Petey jumped down from the statue, but Gabby picked him up again before he could run to the screens. "If you do, then the squid-monster *will* have you," she whispered gently.

On the screen, Blinzarra seemed to be speaking similarly to Petey's dad in a similarly soothing manner. She leaned close to the small man, her head larger than his whole body. "Please, Lester," she said. "I'll get Petey back along with Sharli and Sneakers. I promise."

Petey's dad, Lester, looked at Blinzarra with fury in his eyes. His lips were pursed and his hands balled into fists ... but he nodded stoically and walked down the conference table, out of the shot. Blinzarra sat back down, and the squid-creature with the mustache spoke to her urgently.

"Blinzarra, this Esquagonian is acting as a rogue agent," he said. "Our planetary government did *not* sanction this kidnapping."

"You didn't need to," Blinzarra said, her voice thrumming with fury. "You knew someone on Esquagon would step up and do it for you. Of course they would—you've made sure every Esquagonian hates all Miravlads. So when a 'rogue agent' took my baby, you could act innocent, like you came here in good faith, but you did *not*. I should press this button right now!"

Blinzarra raised her hand over what Gabby now noticed was a large red button near the end of the table, but another creature raced into view and pointed at Blinzarra's wrist. Blinzarra's arm stopped short as if it were suddenly made of stone. The creature was vaguely human-shaped but covered in bright orange fur and had a duck beak, big googly eyes, and bunny ears. It looked more like a sports team mascot than any kind of leader, but when it locked eyes with Blinzarra, it was clear that this creature was not to be trifled with.

"I won't keep you like this against your will, but let's take a moment to talk before you make any decision you can't take back."

Gabby recognized that voice. It was the same young, female, resonant voice she'd heard in her dream-that-wasn't-a-dream. It was the judge . . . or someone who sounded exactly like her.

Blinzarra nodded. The orange creature must have released her arm because Blinzarra lowered it, tucking it under the table and away from the button.

"I'll talk," she said, "but I guarantee there won't be peace in the universe as long as these . . . these . . . *scaphadrills* are part of it!"

"*Scaphadrills?!*" the mustached squid screamed, then he and Blinzarra both stood and shouted at each other. Petey's dad quickly joined the fray, then more aliens crowded into the shot and screamed across the table, taking sides and talking on top of one another until nothing Gabby heard made any sense at all.

"Wow," Petey said. He had climbed up onto the statue to get a better view.

"Petey, what are they talking about?" Gabby asked. "What's going on over there?"

196

"I'll tell you what's going on," Petey said with a wide grin. "Blinzarra said the *S*-word! She's gonna be *so mad* when she finds out I know. And do you see my dad? He's hard-core kragphemous! Look at him, swinging off that Esquagonian's mustache. You tell him, Dad!"

Despite the circumstances, Gabby had to smile. Petey's dad had leaped onto the squid-alien's mustache and swung up to the top of his head, where he was now jumping up and down and screaming at the creature. Clearly, Petey had gotten his acrobatics and fearlessness from his father.

"He is pretty kragphemous," Gabby agreed, "but I meant what's going on *there*, with all the aliens on the screen? I thought your dad and Blinzarra were at a P.T.A. meeting."

"They are," Petey said. "The Planetary Treaty Association. P.T.A."

It took a second for that to sink in. When it did, she almost forgot to whisper. "Ohhhhhh! *That's* the P.T.A.! That's why the meeting was so important. But who's the pink squid? And why did *this* pink squid bring Sharli and Sneakers to Mars?"

"I dunno why Mars, but the squid probably took Sharli and Sneakers 'cause he's an Esquagonian. And it's like Blinzarra said: Esquagonians hate Miravlads. They have for eons. It started when they both discovered the same planet—Blartnok 939—at the same time. They both put settlements there, and they both said it was theirs. They've been fighting ever since. You wanna know the big reason Mars has to keep making more and more kragphemous weapons? 'Cause Esquagon and Miravlad keep asking for bigger and cooler things to use against each other."

Gabby pulled a curl around and tucked it into her mouth, sucking on it as she thought. "Okay . . . but if this is a Planetary *Treaty* Association meeting, does that mean they're going to stop fighting?"

"Uh-huh. It's a big deal 'cause Esquagon and Miravlad are a couple galaxies away from each other, so when they fight, all these other planets get caught up in it, too. So all these ambassadors from planets around the universe, like my dad, stepped in to help them figure things out, and it worked. They called a cease-fire—all the battles on these other screens have to be from the way Outer Reaches—and said they'd meet on Earth to finish working it all out and sign this huge treaty. But if either Blinzarra or the Esquagonian ambassador presses the big red button, that's the signal the peace is over. They'll fight even harder, and more galaxies'll be drawn in. It'll spread through the whole universe, but the galaxy that'll be in the biggest trouble right away is the Milky Way."

"The Milky Way?" Gabby asked. "That's my galaxy. Earth's galaxy."

"Ex-galaxy," Petey said. "If the peace doesn't work out. That's another reason the P.T.A. meeting's on Earth. My dad says it's supposed to help everyone see some of what's at stake."

Gabby looked back at the giant screen, where all the ambassadors were shouting and fighting, and her stomach went hollow. She knew it wasn't right—that war and devastation for *any* creatures should upset her—but knowing Earth was at stake still made it a million times worse.

Gabby looked at Petey. "Are you sure?"

Petey rolled his eyes. "Are you kidding? My mom and dad talk about this *alllllll* the time." Then he grinned. "You really think he's gonna tear up the universe for me?"

"I bet he definitely would," Gabby said. "But maybe we can get you, Sharli, and Sneakers home safe so he doesn't have to."

Petey nodded and went back to watching the fracas on the screen. Gabby watched it, too, but she was scanning the crowd for Edwina. Was she there at the P.T.A. meeting? And if everyone knew Petey, Sneakers, and Sharli were gone, did they know Gabby was gone, too? Maybe the ambassadors wouldn't know, but Edwina would, right? She always seemed to know where Gabby was and what she was doing. Plus Edwina knew Sharli was in danger—she had warned Gabby about it—so if Edwina saw the video of the Esquagonian with Sharli and Sneakers, that would be a good thing. She'd know her suspicions were right, and she'd know where to come save her.

Gabby frowned as she realized that wasn't true. The Martians weren't visible on the video feed. If Edwina saw it, she wouldn't think the Martians were involved at all, just the Esquagonians. If she were arranging some kind of rescue, she'd arrange it on Esquagon, the wrong planet.

But why *were* the Martians involved? It didn't make sense. Gabby twirled a curl around her finger as she thought about it.

"You said the Martians gave weapons to Esquagon *and* Miravlad," Gabby whispered to Petey. "So why are they helping an Esquagonian hold Sharli and Sneakers? And why are they keeping it a secret from the P.T.A.?"

Petey shrugged. "Beats me."

Just then, Sharli and Sneakers's giant squid-creature kidnapper growled into the camera. "Looks like you have a lot to discuss," he told the P.T.A. "We'll leave you to it. Keep this channel open, Blinzarra, but remember, my demands are clear. The Miravlads must vacate Blartnok 939 immediately, and sign a treaty giving all rights to the planet, now and forever, to Esquagon. Do that, or you'll never see your daughter, or your dog, again."

Gabby saw Blinzarra turn back to the camera, her face desperate as she cried, "No!" She said more, but Gabby couldn't hear it. The squid-creature had muted her feed. He'd also turned off his own. Gabby could see the image in the corner—what Blinzarra was seeing on her side—had gone black. Blinzarra kept shouting into the camera for a bit—at least it looked like she was shouting. Petey's dad was shouting at the camera, too, even as he continued to jump up and down on the Esquagonian ambassador's head. Then Blinzarra turned back to the Esquagonian ambassador, channeling all her fury toward him. He looked just as livid.

It was not looking good for peace in the universe . . . or for the future of Earth.

chapter
SEVENTEEN

The squid-creature in the room with Gabby turned to the Martians around him. "We'll let them stew for a while," he said. "Take the girl and the dog."

In unison, the three Martians clicked their heels and flapped their bent arms. Gabby supposed it was a salute, but it looked more like the Chicken Dance. Then one of the Martians unhooked Sneakers's leash, while another picked up Sharli. Sharli whimpered and struggled until the Martian gave her a rough shake, and Gabby had to force herself not to run out and tackle the metallic beast herself. Sneakers clearly felt the same way. He snarled and bared his teeth through the muzzle. The Martians ignored him, but Sharli quickly quieted, and the Martians moved toward the door. Gabby crouched lower and curled herself farther behind the statue platform so none of them would see her as they left the room.

"C'mon, Petey," she whispered, patting her shoulder so he'd hop aboard. "Let's follow them."

Gabby didn't feel his weight hopping on her shoulder. In fact, he didn't respond at all.

"Petey?"

Trying to remain silent, Gabby looked frantically around. She even took off her knapsack and unzipped it slowly, so it wouldn't make a noise. Petey wasn't inside. Where was he?

She peeked over the statue platform and scanned the room. What she saw made her heart thunder.

Petey was near the desk. He was climbing on the revolving display case that held the flat bands—the ones Petey said were the Martian's robotic suits.

Gabby couldn't call out. She gestured wildly for him to come back, but he wasn't looking her way. Probably on purpose.

Then she heard a low, grumbling sigh and saw the giant pink squid-creature lumbering up the two steps into the upper office. His constantly undulating tentacles made sucking and popping sounds as he moved.

If he turned the slightest bit to his right, he'd see Petey.

Petey seemed to realize it, too. He scurried to the back side of the rotating display case. Gabby couldn't see him, but she imagined him clinging there, hidden from view. She mentally willed him not to move.

The squid-creature reached the room's large, curved executive desk. He leaned heavily on it with one tentacle. With another, he reached for the back of his neck . . . and started peeling away his skin. Gabby's stomach lurched as a thin, circular flap of flesh lifted off his body, bit by bit.

When the circle peeled all the way off, the squid-creature was gone.

Instead, a tiny, sickly, pale green alien stood on the desk. It its right hand was the pink circle, which now looked much more like an acne wipe than actual skin.

Even if Gabby weren't on another planet, "alien" would be the word she'd automatically use to describe the little creature. In all her time working with A.L.I.E.N., this was the first alien she'd seen that looked like the Earth stereotype. Not only did he have the pale green coloring, but he was also hairless, with enormous black eyes, snake-slits for a nose, and a teeny tiny mouth.

The only difference was that unlike the typical long, thin alien, this one was oddly adorable. It was only a head taller than Petey, with a chubby body, chubby arms and legs that rounded off at the ends with no discernible hands or feet. Its head was perfectly round.

He looked like an alien Pillsbury Doughboy rendered in super-cute Japanese kawaii style.

The alien set the patch on the desk, then rolled out his neck. He yawned, and it was so cute Gabby had to smack a hand over her mouth to stop herself from saying *Awwwww* out loud.

Then the little guy bounce-walked to the far edge of the table and reached out for the spinning display case.

Petey was on that case. If the alien spun it . . .

The doughy alien placed one rounded hand to his lips as he ran the other one along the lines of bands. "Hmmm."

Even the little alien's voice was adorably sweet and high-pitched. Despite her fears, Gabby had to fight the urge to run out and hug him.

Then he spun the rack.

Gabby took a deep breath, ready to scream and distract the little alien . . . but Petey wasn't on the back side of the rack. He must have hopped down just in time.

"Ah, that's the one," the little alien cooed. Bending his rounded hand, he removed one of the bands from the rack and slapped it against his pudgy arm. The band curved on impact, wrapping securely around his limb. Then he leaped off the desk, and in midair he touched a spot on the band.

Instantly, layers of metal unfolded from the band, snapping and growing and sliding all around the tiny alien until his feet thumped to the ground. He was no longer an adorable doughy creature at all, but instead a behemoth of metal—a ten-foot-tall gray-green tank of a creature with a faceless iron skull and thick plates of armor from his head to his toes. He had a jet pack on his back and weapons mounted to his shoulders and legs, and both his arms ended in sharp dagger-claws. The band he'd pulled from the rack was still on his arm, but now it was an armlet above his armored elbow, stretched ten times its size to accommodate the metal giant's girth.

He took a deep breath in, and the sound alone turned Gabby's insides to water.

"MUCH BETTER," he said, shaking the room with his low, brutal voice.

Gabby's heart raced as the pieces snapped into place. The Esquagonian wasn't an Esquagonian at all. He was a Martian, and the pink patch had let him change his shape—the same way patches must have let Martians take Gabby's, Zee's, and Satchel's shapes back on Earth. Now this Martian was letting the P.T.A. believe Esquagon was responsible for taking Sharli and Sneakers . . . but why?

The hulking Martian turned and looked at the screen where Blinzarra and the Esquagonian ambassador were still silently fighting. "THAT'S RIGHT," he said with a mirthless chuckle. "KEEP FIGHTING EACH OTHER. GO BACK TO YOUR WAR AND MAKE MARS GREAT AND PROFITABLE AGAIN."

Gabby's eyes widened. She remembered what Petey had said. *You wanna know the big reason Mars has to keep making more and more kragphemous weapons? 'Cause Esquagon and Miravlad keep asking for bigger and cooler things to use against each other.*

Mars wanted the peace talks to fail so they could keep selling weapons. They kidnapped Blinzarra's daughter and framed Esquagon so the two planets would keep fighting! It was the only thing that made sense . . . but there was no one she could tell.

She peered at the giant curved screen on the wall of monitors. She couldn't hear the P.T.A. meeting, but she could see things hadn't gotten better. Everyone was still screaming at one another, and Blinzarra and the Esquagonian with the mustache both kept reaching for the red button. If one of them actually pressed it, the war would be back on. The whole universe would be in danger, with her own planet in the cross fire.

If only there was a way she could turn on the feed and show the P.T.A. the truth . . . But how would she sneak past the beast-tank of a Martian?

207

With heavy thuds, the Martian stomped to the wall of screens. Now she definitely couldn't get to them. Gabby didn't see the Martian touch anything, but he must have done something, because the screen images shifted. Blinzarra and the P.T.A. moved to one of the smaller screens, while the hulking Martian aired one battle scene after another on the bigger one. The carnage seemed to relax him. "YES . . . VERY NICE . . ." he intoned in a low growl.

It was like he was purring.

"I've seen that before," Petey said in her ear.

Gabby gasped. She hadn't even felt him land, but he was on her shoulder. "Petey!"

He continued as if he'd been there all along. "It's from the War of the Yabukerants in the Nubrellian Era. He's not watching stuff from the Outer Reaches at all; he's watching old battles."

"We need to go," Gabby said. "Come on."

Gabby had an idea, but they needed to move quickly and get out of the office while the hulking Martian was still engrossed in his screens. She slid out from behind the statue's pedestal and peered through the doorway. Three Martians—they looked like the same three who'd just taken Sneakers and Sharli—entered the circular walkway from the hall containing the prison cells, then went into one of the other rooms. Gabby gave them a moment to walk out of earshot, then slipped into the corridor herself and edged along the wall, away from the now-giant Martian's office. She took Petey off her shoulder so she could look at him while she spoke.

"The transport pods," she whispered. "You said you had a VR thing that let you go in and program them. Think you could program the real thing?"

"Uh, yeah," Petey said immediately. "The *R* in VR is 'reality.' If I can do it in VR, I can do it in real life."

"Okay," Gabby said. "Then the plan is we get Sneakers and Sharli, we go to the pods, and you get us back to Earth. Then we can tell the P.T.A. that the Martians took Sneakers and Sharli, not the Esquagonians. We'll save the peace talks, save Earth, and save the universe."

"Cool," Petey said, sounding much less impressed than Gabby thought he might, given the epic adventure she'd just laid out. "Aren't you gonna ask me where I was?"

"In the office? I know where you were. I saw you. You were trying to get a Metall-O-Band."

"Yeah, but I didn't, 'cause mini-Martian came over before I could. I mean after that. Aren't you gonna ask me?"

Gabby scrunched her brows. She was pretty sure he came over to her and jumped on her shoulder after that. "Okay . . . where were you?"

"I came over to you and jumped on your shoulder," he said.

He could clearly tell he was getting Gabby exasperated, because he finished his thought quickly. "But on the way I grabbed *this*."

He held up the pink acne pad—the one the Martian had peeled off the back of his neck.

Gabby gasped. "What are you doing with that?!"

"Well, I wanted to get *something*. And this is cool. Look!"

He wriggled out of Gabby's hands, ran up her arm, then slid down her jacket and landed on the floor. Standing in front of her, he slapped the pink patch on the back of his neck, and instantly morphed into the same eight-foot-tall pink squid-creature with all the writhing tentacles that they'd just seen in the office.

"Ta-da!" Petey cried in the squid-creature's grumbling voice.

"Are you crazy?!" Gabby snapped. She reached up and snatched the pink patch off the back of his neck, turning Petey immediately back to himself. "Are you trying to get us caught? He's going to want this when he talks to Blinzarra again! What do you think he'll do when he sees it's gone?"

Petey bit his lip, abashed. "Wonder if someone took it?"

"Yes! Wonder if someone took it! And then he'll look for *who* took it, and bad things will happen!"

"Right," Petey said. Then he brightened. "What if I put it back where I found it?"

Gabby shook her head. "Too dangerous. If he decides he wants it while you're still there, you could get caught. Let's just hurry and get Sneakers and Sharli, then go to the pod. I'll hold on to this."

She slipped one arm out of its knapsack strap and swung the bag around so she could put the patch in a front pouch. Then she put her hand out and Petey hopped into it. After she listened closely to make sure no one was coming, Gabby darted to the prison area's archway. She didn't know for sure Sneakers and Sharli were there, but it seemed like their best bet. It *was* a prison, after all, and they'd seen the other Martians coming out of it.

Gabby tried not to dwell on the fact that if she was wrong, she and Petey wouldn't be the only ones in trouble. The whole universe would pay the price.

chapter
EIGHTEEN

the only light inside the prison hall came from the laser mesh blocking each cell, which bathed everything in an eerie red glow. Gabby had no idea how many cells snaked through the halls, or how many held prisoners. She had no idea if it was an actual prison for Martians who broke the law, or a place where the Martians only brought outsiders, like Sharli and Sneakers.

What she did know was that she didn't have time to check every cell, which meant she needed Sneakers's help. She moved deep enough into the main hallway that no one in the outside corridor could see her, then pressed herself against a wall between two cells, blending into the shadows. She closed her eyes and concentrated.

Where are you, Sneakers? She thought it with all her might. *Where are you?*

She expected Sneakers to show her another vision.

Instead the dog whined, which made Gabby realize Sneakers was much smarter than her. The halls all looked exactly the same—red lasers and cells. A vision would have done her no good at all.

Sneakers kept whining—not constantly, but just often enough that Gabby could follow the sound. It led her down a labyrinth of halls, through which she moved painfully slowly. She desperately wanted to run, but she couldn't risk anyone hearing her pounding feet, so she tiptoed, and neither she nor Petey said a word. As she searched, she stretched out with her ears, listening for metallic footsteps, but none came. She did hear low growls coming from several cells, but they never got louder as Gabby walked by. That was good, but it didn't put her at ease. Every nerve in Gabby's body was at full attention; the strain made her sweat like she was running a marathon.

Finally, Sneakers's cries were just ahead. Gabby stopped before she reached his cell, then edged in front of it.

In the dim light from the laser beam lattice, she saw them: Sneakers and Sharli. They were on a tall metal podium in the middle of a square room otherwise devoid of furniture. Sharli sat, while Sneakers lay curled around her. The top of the podium was so small there was barely any extra space around him. Sneakers was still muzzled, but the Martians had taken off Sharli's blindfold. She sucked her thumb and curled the fingers of her other hand through Sneakers's fur. She looked so sad it broke Gabby's heart.

More low growls came from either side of the podium. Two snarling beasts stood guard over Sharli and Sneakers, and Gabby realized similar beasts must be in every cell with prisoners; that's why the growling haunted the halls. The beasts were unlike any animals Gabby had ever seen. They had the bodies of lions, but lions who hit the gym every day. Their eyes glowed red, with no pupils at all. Their heavy brows extended beyond their faces, curving up into thick, sharp horns. Their mouths dripped with foam, through which Gabby could see their razor-sharp teeth and upper and lower fangs. Their paws ended in nails so thick and pointed, Gabby imagined they could puncture sheets of steel as if they were tissue paper.

The animals stared at Sharli and Sneakers, never taking their eyes off the prisoners for a second, their bodies tensed and ready to pounce.

"What do we do, Gabby?" Petey whispered.

Gabby's skin prickled, but the clearly well-trained beasts

didn't respond to the sound of his voice. Sharli, however, looked up.

"Pe-ey!" she called around the thumb in her mouth. "Ga-ee!"

She stood and reached out her arms, and the movement triggered the guard beasts. They barked and snarled, spittle flying, and the echoes of their roars bounced off the cell walls. Sharli squealed, terrified, and sat back down, where Sneakers curled even more tightly around her.

Once she was seated, the beasts quieted. They went back to their positions: tense, watching, and constantly on alert.

"Soooo, the savage bodybuilder lion dogs," Petey said after a long moment. "They're a problem."

Gabby almost laughed. They had a whole bunch of problems right now. The rapacious monster dogs might not even make the top of the list. "They're two of our problems, yeah," Gabby said, "but they won't matter if we can't get past the lasers."

"That's easy. We did it before. I put on the springs, bounce up, use the mirror, and stop the laser." He thought a second, then added, "Got any Minisculean-sized gloves in your bag? I don't wanna get burned."

"I don't, but it doesn't matter," Gabby said. "That won't work this time."

She knew because she had been thinking the same thing

and had already pulled the lip gloss compact out of her jacket pocket. She showed it to Petey. The mirror was hopelessly cracked from its fall after Petey dropped it outside the tower. Several chunks were missing.

"Okay, so we won't use that," Petey said. "Got any other mirrors?"

Gabby didn't, but even if she did, it wouldn't help. She'd been staring at the cell, and she now saw the source of the laser gate. Unlike the one outside the tower, there was no telescoping ledge on which Petey could stand and hold the mirror. The cell's arched opening was lined in sheer metal, and the laser eye projector was built into it, flush with that metal. There was no good way Petey could get up to it and block it—nothing for him to hold on to. And while Gabby was sure Zee could think of a million different ways to do it—like shooting some kind of rope up to the ceiling and having Petey swing to the laser eye—it wouldn't be even remotely safe, and Gabby wouldn't risk Petey getting vaporized for a one-in-a-million chance of success.

She explained the situation to Petey, but he was undeterred. "Okay, but I can still get in there," he said. "It's the same lasers as outside. I can fit through the holes and get Sneakers and Sharli out."

"Get them out how?" Gabby asked. "They can't fit

through like you. We still need to shut down the lasers. We just need another way."

Gabby racked her brain, but she couldn't think of anything. Then Sneakers raised his head and looked her straight in the eye.

The next thing Gabby knew, she was looking at the latticed laser wall from *inside* the cell. Three Martians approached, then Gabby's vision moved to the monster dogs, who perked up as if they'd heard something. Gabby realized she was seeing them from up high, as if she were on the podium looking down at them—like Sneakers. The ravening brutes looked toward the Martians on the other side of the lasers and panted and wagged their tails, for this one moment looking more like dogs than beasts. The Sneakers-vision followed them as they trotted toward a small black circle along a side wall. One of the lion-dog-beasts reared back on its hind legs, put its paws on the wall, and ran its tongue over the circle.

Right away, the vision panned back to the entrance of the cell.

The laser mesh was gone, and the three Martian guards walked in.

". . . so once we find a Shrink-O-Zapper and steal it . . ." Petey said. He sounded like he'd been talking awhile—maybe even the whole time—but Gabby hadn't heard a word of it.

"Petey, stop," she said. "Sneakers showed me something—something he saw before." She squinted her eyes and peered into the cell. The small black circle was there on the side wall, exactly where it had been in Sneakers's vision.

"Okay," Petey said. "What did he show you?"

"How to turn the lasers off. They're controlled by a lickpad."

"A *lickpad*?" Petey echoed. "That's not even a thing."

"It is here. When the guards come, they signal to the dog beasts, and they lick that pad to turn off the lasers."

"That's gross."

"How is that gross?" Gabby asked. "They're animals. Animals lick."

"Okay, then it's just weird."

"It's not," Gabby said, thinking about it out loud, "not if the Martians are afraid of people like us helping prisoners from outside the cell. The guard dogs are trained; they only open the door for the right signal."

"Cool. Then give 'em the signal."

Gabby shook her head. "Sneakers couldn't tell me the signal. It's a sound. I only saw what Sneakers saw; I couldn't hear what he heard."

"Okay ..." Petey said, thinking it through, "but animals lick, right? Like you said. So *Sneakers* can lick the door open!"

Sneakers perked his head up, like he'd heard exactly what Petey had said. He gave the boy a knowing gaze. Then, keeping himself curled around Sharli, he stretched one paw off the edge of the podium.

The guard beasts roared to life, leaping up toward the podium as they snarled and barked, spittle flying everywhere. Sneakers quickly withdrew his paw and the monster-dogs settled back into their stiff-bodied watch.

"Or not," Petey said.

"We need another way to get the guard monsters to lick the pad," Gabby said, "but it has to be something that'll keep them busy long enough for Sneakers and Sharli to get out."

"It's too bad the lickpad isn't a bone," Petey said. "When Sneakers has a bone, he spends all day with it. And he licks it, too. Licks it, chews it, carries it around with him till it gets all gross and wet and slobbery . . ."

Sneakers thumped his tail against the podium. Even the word "bone" made him happy. Unfortunately, Gabby had no way to turn the lickpad into a bone. She also didn't carry dog bones with her unless she knew ahead of time she was babysitting for a kid with a dog.

She *did* carry Satchel's pizza-dough breadsticks. Would the guard beasts like those?

Gabby slid off her knapsack and knelt down to unzip it. The second it was open, the creatures' wide nostrils began to twitch. The beasts remained on alert, muscles tensed and bodies pointed at the top of the podium . . . but their eyes kept darting toward Gabby. And the sniffing got louder.

Could they smell the breadsticks? It seemed unlikely; the breadsticks were in their sealed plastic container. Gabby couldn't smell them at all. The only thing she could smell was . . .

"The fish sticks!" she cried.

She yanked the napkin-wrapped parcel out of her knapsack, and the guard dogs went crazy. They broke away from their stations on either side of the podium and ran at the lattice gate. They stopped just short of it and barked ferociously, lunging and snapping and spraying spittle that sizzled into oblivion on the lasers.

Gabby felt Petey scramble to take refuge on top of her head. "They really want those fish sticks, Gabby! I think you should let them have 'em!"

"Not yet," Gabby said. "We need to use the fish sticks to get Sharli and Sneakers out!"

"But they could lick the pad to get rid of the gate right now! Then they'll eat us *and* the fish sticks!"

Gabby shook her head. Gently, so she didn't dislodge Petey. The dogs' gnashing, rapacious teeth scared her, too, but she stayed calm for Petey's sake and told him what she hoped was the truth. "I don't think they're smart enough," she said. "If they were, they'd have opened it already. They only lick the pad when they get the signal. But I bet they'd lick it for these."

Gabby opened the napkin to reveal six fish sticks, and the dog beasts went even wilder. More foam, more snapping, those horns that could rip her apart with a single stroke. Gabby was glad an array of lasers separated her and Petey from them. She couldn't believe she was about to purposely take it away.

She had to move quickly. She now understood it was normal for the cell beasts to bark and roar whenever prisoners moved, but if these two kept going, any Martians in the section might hear them and get suspicious.

"What are you gonna do?" Petey asked, his voice growing higher as the frantic beasts jumped and yelped. "Throw the fish sticks at the lickpad? They won't stick!"

"That's why I won't throw them," Gabby said. Then she called, "Wanna play a game, Sharli? We can be puppies on a mission, like your show this morning."

Despite the barking and frothing, Sharli looked intrigued. Her braids clacked as she tilted her head, curious. "Pa-pee?"

Gabby nodded and forced her voice not to quaver. "Uh-huh." She held out her cupped hands, full of the fish sticks. "All we need are these fish sticks on that little black circle. But don't let them touch the red lines in front of me, okay? And don't let the mean dogs eat them until the fish sticks are *on* the circle."

Sharli furrowed her brow, taking it very seriously. "No red. No eat." Then she called out, trying to sound like the show, "Pa-pee Gard—go!"

She stared at the fish sticks, and they soared out of Gabby's hands and threaded themselves through different holes high in the laser mesh.

The guard beasts stopped barking. They leaped and snapped, desperate to catch the treats. They had amazing vertical power, jumping halfway to the ceiling to try to grab their snack, but Sharli kept whooshing the fish sticks just out of their reach. Then she dive-bombed the fish sticks onto the lickpad, where she mushed them all around.

Instantly, the beasts were on them, and the very first lick made the laser mesh disappear. In a moment of sheer terror, Gabby worried that the licking would turn *on* the lasers, too, but deep down she knew better—Sneakers wouldn't have shown her the image if she'd only succeed in strobing the deadly lasers on and off.

Keeping one eye on the dog beasts, who had scarfed down the fish sticks in an instant but kept snuffling around and licking up the last remnants of grease, Gabby raced into the cell and grabbed Sharli. The instant Gabby had her, Sneakers jumped off the podium, ran out of the cell, and down the hall. Gabby didn't need him to look back to know he wanted her to follow.

Gabby felt to make sure Petey was still on her head. "Hold on, Petey!"

She ran after Sneakers as fast as she could while holding Sharli. The little girl's braids bounced and smacked Gabby in the face as they went, but Gabby was happy to take the abuse if it meant getting out of the prison hall quickly.

On her own, Gabby would have gotten hopelessly lost, but Sneakers knew every twist and turn through the maze of red laser-lit halls. He wound through them fast enough to push Gabby to her limits but never so fast that she lost sight of his swishing brown-and-white tail. This time Gabby didn't worry about her feet pounding on the floor. Now that she had Sharli and Sneakers, all she wanted to do was get to a transport pod and get back home as fast as possible.

It wasn't until Gabby finally saw the stark-white light of the circular corridor up ahead that she heard snarling, foamy, slobbery roars and the pounding of heavy feet and claws behind them.

The guard beasts had come after them.

chapter
NINETEEN

*G*abby's heart jumped into her throat.

From the bellowing and howling, she knew the creatures were angry. Luckily, they were also still far away. Gabby had to move fast; if the beasts got close enough, they'd rip her, Sneakers, Sharli, and Petey to shreds.

"Wait for me at the door!" Gabby called to Sneakers between panting breaths. "I know where we're going!"

Sneakers did as he was told. The dog waited just inside the doorway and looked back at Gabby, wagging his tail anxiously. Gabby poured on speed and burst out of the doorway and into the circular hall. She had so much momentum she had to hold Sharli out of the way as her side slammed hard into the elevator, which complained with a loud metallic *BONG*.

"WHAT WAS THAT?!"

The low, horrible roar froze Gabby in place. She knew the voice. It was the Martian from the executive office, the one who had disguised himself as an Esquagonian.

A moment later he called out again, but this cry was far worse, and so loud it shook the entire hallway. "WHERE IS MY MO-EMULATOR PATCH??!!"

Gabby hadn't heard the term before, but she knew what he was after. He'd just realized the pink patch that turned him into an Esquagonian was gone. And the thundering footsteps that echoed into the hall meant he was coming to look for it.

"The transport pods!" Gabby whisper-hissed to Sneakers.

Sneakers understood and slipped inside the pod room's arched entryway. Holding Sharli close, and with Petey grasping her shoulder, Gabby darted after him.

She almost made it.

BLAM! Gabby screamed and jumped back as an orange beam zapped across her path. The beam hit the door jamb and turned it into dripping tar.

"YOU!"

The Martian's booming voice was far too close. He had come out of his office and now stood just around the circular hall from Gabby. He still wore the massive armored tank of a suit, and though his metallic-slab head had no facial features, Gabby could feel his baleful glare. One of his shoulder weapons still steamed from its tar-laser blast. The other one pivoted, aiming right at Gabby's face. She jumped back just as the weapon zapped to life.

It turned the edge of the elevator shaft to ice.

"YOU THINK YOU CAN GET AWAY?!" the Martian roared.

His voice turned Gabby to jelly, but she couldn't give in to her fear. She edged herself farther around the circular hallway until the elevator shaft blocked him entirely. If she couldn't see him, he couldn't see her. And he couldn't blast her either.

From the room with the prison cells, Gabby heard the guard-creatures snarling and growling. Voices and footsteps echoed from the other rooms. Any second now the hall would teem with Martians and ravenous beasts, and Gabby would have no hope of getting to the transport pods.

Gabby heard a high-pitched electric whine as the entire top of the elevator shaft glowed bright yellow, then vanished. With her cover disintegrated, Gabby was now face-to-face with the Martian. One of his leg blasters steamed, and both shoulder blasters pointed right at her. He had no mouth, but his voice smiled unctuously.

"PEEK-A-BOO."

Gabby devoted exactly one millisecond to wondering if he'd gotten the term from Earth visits or if peek-a-boo was really that universal, then Petey dove into her hair while Sharli whimpered and hid her head against Gabby's pounding chest. Gabby pulled her in and tried to turn her away from the laser blast that was sure to come.

"WHHHOOOOOAAAA!!!!"

The giant, hulking Martian hollered out loud as he tumbled forward, toppling into the remains of the elevator shaft.

Stunned, Gabby watched him fall, then looked up and saw Sneakers. He was standing where the Martian had just been, wagging his tail proudly.

"You pushed him!" Petey called from atop Gabby's head. "Good dog!"

"*Strong* dog," Gabby said. "That suit is *heavy*."

WHOOSH!

Gabby looked down the elevator shaft, to the source of the sound. The falling Martian had stopped falling, and was now rocketing back up toward them.

"His jet pack!" Petey cried.

The footsteps and dog snarls were louder now, too. Their enemies were closing in from every direction.

Confident that Sneakers would follow, Gabby dove into the transport pod room and immediately ducked into one directly to the left—the same one she and Petey had hidden behind earlier. Sneakers zipped in beside her as Gabby put Sharli down, grabbed the door handle, and heaved her body backward to slide the heavy metal panel shut. She heard a satisfying click and hoped that meant it was locked.

"Petey," Gabby panted, "can you get us to Earth?"

"Uh-huh," he said. He had already jumped away from Gabby and was climbing around on a wall full of cogs, gears, levers, buttons, and monitors. Gabby couldn't make sense out of any of it, but Petey raced up and down the wall using all his limbs at once. He flipped switches with his elbows, ran on dials to turn them, then bounced down to type on a keyboard filled with characters Gabby's translator stripe couldn't even decipher. "Easiest way is to go right back to the portal we came through to get here."

The machine started to hum. The sound was low, and above it she could still hear footsteps. They clacked all around the transport pod now, like raindrops in a driving storm.

Gabby knelt down and tried to take off Sneakers's muzzle, but she couldn't. Her whole body was shaking. Her fingers kept slipping off the buckles.

"Hurry, Petey," she urged.

The door of the transport pod started to rattle.

"Almost ready," Petey said. He stretched to reach something with his left arm.

"What are you trying to get?" Gabby asked. "I can—"

SWOOSH!

The pod door flew open and the executive office Martian squeezed inside the pod. His hulking metal body filled the entryway, but through the few cracks of light around him Gabby could see an army of smaller Martians, as well as the snarling, frothing guard dogs.

There was a whirr as the Martian's tank-like armor shifted and opened out to reveal countless weapons, every one of which spun to face Gabby.

As more and more weapons unfolded, Gabby's ears throbbed with the rush of her blood roaring in her veins.

This was it. This was how she was going to die—disintegrated by an adorable alien marshmallow puff in a big metal suit.

An adorable alien marshmallow puff . . .

Gabby broke out in goose bumps. How had she not thought about this until now?

"Sharli," Gabby whispered. "The band on his right arm, above his elbow. *Now!*"

Gabby saw the flash as every weapon on the Martian's body fired at her . . . but each laser beam and blaster bolt fizzled in midair as the band snapped off the Martian's arm and his entire monster-tank of a suit instantly disappeared, leaving only the rounded pillow of pudgy white-green alien cuteness standing on the floor.

Outside the transport pod's open door, the crowd of Martians looked down and gasped. Even the dog beasts stopped snarling and stared.

"Great and Powerful Eminence," a stunned Martian in charcoal armor said. "You're *tiny!*"

The chubby little Martian's huge eyes got even huger as he looked down at himself, his sweet little mouth a perfect O.

"No-no-no-no-*no!*" he squeaked. Then he ran to Gabby and hid behind her leg. "Close the door! Close it!"

Gabby didn't hesitate. While the army of Martians outside were still gaping, she lunged to the handle and heaved the door shut. The click of the lock seemed to jolt the crowd, and the door immediately started to rattle. Gabby knew the Martians would pull it back open any second.

"Petey?" Gabby called.

"Almost!" Petey cried back as he jumped across a keypad. He landed with his legs straddled, pressing two buttons at once, then leaned back to reach for another control.

"How dare you do this to me in front of my subjects!" a tiny voice screamed.

Gabby wheeled around just in time to see a white-green blur, as the Marshmallow Peep of a Martian sprang up and grabbed Gabby's face. He clung to the sides of her head with his legs, pummeling her forehead with his pillowy fists.

It's like getting attacked by an angry cotton ball, Gabby thought.

It was the last thing to cross her mind before the door latch opened . . . then everything disappeared.

chapter
TWENTY

PLOOSH!

The next thing Gabby knew, she was lying on her back in a pool of sticky goo, and everything smelled like pizza.

She turned her head, and her cheek smushed down into more goo.

It didn't just smell like pizza, it *was* pizza.

"Gabby?"

The incredulous voice belonged to Alice. Gabby lifted her head and saw her mom across a sea of cheese and pepperoni. Her eyes were wide, and her hands were on her face. Arlington was right next to her, frozen in open-mouthed shock. As Gabby looked around, she saw nothing but people, standing in a wide circle, all gaping at her . . . while she was surrounded by pizza.

Gabby's blood chilled as she realized where she was: smack in the middle of the world's largest pizza, with hundreds of people gathered around her.

But was she alone?

She spun onto her knees, ignoring the sauce and cheese that seeped through her jeans. "Sharli? Sneakers? Petey?"

She frantically sloshed in a circle until she saw them. They were all there, sprawled out in different spots on the giant pizza. Sharli sat cross-legged, splashing down her hands, then giggling as she raised them up again, stretching lengths of gooey cheese; Sneakers rolled around on his back in the toppings, coating his fur in goo. Petey whooped as he leaped from pepperoni to pepperoni, as if the meat slices were stepping stones.

Gabby was so relieved, she didn't even realize the ramifications of what was happening—that she had literally just appeared out of nowhere in the middle of a giant pizza with a dog, a toddler, and a human being the size of a box of crayons.

Then she heard the scream.

"ALIEN!!!!"

It was Madison Murray. She stood right next to Dina Parker, the reporter, and Dina's cameraman, who looked like he was filming. It didn't surprise Gabby that Madison had tracked down Dina and planted herself by her side. What did surprise her was the subject of Madison's scream. It wasn't Sneakers, Petey, or Sharli . . . it was the Martian. The adorably chubby white-green creature with huge black pupil-less eyes and slits for a nose bounded across the pizza. His mouth and brow were furrowed in a sneer, but the fierce gaze somehow only made him look cuter. Sauce splashed in his wake as he ran toward Gabby.

With a sweetly high-pitched samurai scream, he leaped into the air and latched on to Gabby's sauce-stained purple puffer jacket. He pummeled her chest with his fists, which felt like getting beaten with cotton candy. In other words, she couldn't feel a thing.

She couldn't *feel* a thing . . . but she could see and hear everything.

The shock that had silenced the crowd had worn off. What sounded like a million voices were shouting, and what looked like a zillion cell phones were pointed at her and the most alien-looking alien Gabby had ever seen.

"This is Dina Parker, coming to you *live* from the fair, where we are currently witnessing a genuine alien invasion. Get a close-up, Charlie."

"Yes!" cried Madison. She jumped onto the pizza so she could stand right in front of the cameraman. "And get a close-up of *me*, Madison Murray, whose very best friend, Gabby Duran, is in the pizza with the alien. I'll tell you everything you need to know, Dina."

Gabby's head spun. She hadn't just broken A.L.I.E.N.'s number one rule, she'd demolished it. Proof of alien life was right now being blasted to people's TVs. It didn't matter that Dina was only local news—something like this would be picked up nationally. *Inter*nationally. It would go viral. Everyone would see it, including G.E.T.O.U.T. and all the other enemies of aliens here on Earth. Every family Gabby had met, every kid she'd ever babysat, they'd be in horrible danger now, and it was all her fault.

Gabby tried to fix it. She whipped off her knapsack and pulled out her fake remote control. She feverishly pressed its buttons and wrangled its joystick. "Look at me!" she said loudly, right into the camera. "I'm remote-controlling these alien toys!"

Looking at the camera might not have been the best idea. It took her eyes off the small Martian, who yanked the remote out of her hands and hurled it behind him. Then he hopped onto Gabby's head and furiously jumped up and down. It felt like a light drizzle.

The remote *thwocked* into Zee's stomach as she and Satchel ran across the pizza toward Gabby. Zee *oofed* as it hit her but quickly recovered and picked up where Gabby left off.

"Oooh!" she shouted in the most stilted voice Gabby had ever heard. "Thanks, Gabs, for getting your *toy* to throw this to me! Now I'm totally controlling this wild, seemingly alien craziness!"

She lowered her voice as she and Satchel reached Gabby. They crouched over her, speaking over each other in soft, urgent tones.

"We're so sorry," Zee said. "We were gonna leave the rock where it was."

"But we didn't want anyone else to take it," Satchel said. "And my aunt Toni found us."

"They put that app on Satchel's phone," Zee added, "the one that always tells them where he is."

"It's for work!" Satchel said defensively. "For pizza deliveries. And I left it on today 'cause I didn't know we'd be with you and the you-know-whats."

Zee rolled her eyes. "Whatever. She found us and she made us help with the pizza."

"You know Aunt Toni," Satchel said. "You can't say no to her."

"So I put the rock in my pocket," Zee said. "Just to keep it safe."

"And we were gonna take it back where we found it, I swear—"

"But it got super hot—like it was *burning* my overalls. So I took it out, but I had to bobble it around 'cause it burned—"

"But it was blinking purple, and I didn't want anyone to see, so I grabbed it!" Satchel snapped his fist around an imaginary rock to illustrate. Then he winced and looked down, abashed. Zee furrowed her brow sympathetically and put a hand on his arm.

"He didn't mean it," she said to Gabby. "The rock was seriously hot. It burned his hand."

"I wasn't even thinking," Satchel said. "I just threw it . . . and it landed in the middle of the pizza. And then . . ."

"Excuse me!"

Dina Parker's strident voice cut through everything else. She edged next to Gabby, pushing Zee and Satchel aside. Then she turned to the camera and flashed a megawatt smile. "Dina Parker here, back with the alien from another planet. Tell us, alien . . . tell the people of Earth, why are you here? Would you like us to take you to our leader?"

237

While Satchel and Zee were talking, the Martian had stopped jumping on Gabby's head. He now braced his feet against Gabby's chest, held the edges of her unzipped jacket, and head-butted her in the throat. It was like getting pounded by dandelion fluff.

Yet when the Martian heard Dina's question, he froze. He looked at Dina . . . looked at her microphone . . . looked at the camera . . . then his eyes rounded and pooled with tears. Somehow he managed to look even smaller and cuter than before.

"It was terrible," he said in his tiny, high voice. He looked right into the lens. His little lips quivered. "The Esquagonians . . . they kidnapped me! They kidnapped all of us! Me, the human, the Miravlad . . . all of us! It was terrible!"

He burst into adorable tears and buried his face in Gabby's jacket.

"Awwww," Zee and Satchel chorused.

"No!" Gabby objected. "No 'aw'! That's not what happened at all! This alien is from Mars—not *that* Mars, and—"

Gabby was cut off by the roar of an engine. A black limousine was racing across the pizza. With a *scree* of brakes, it fishtailed to a stop mere inches from Gabby, spraying cheese, pepperoni, and sauce all over her, the Martian, Zee, Satchel, and Dina.

"My pantsuit!" Dina wailed.

The back door of the limousine opened. Edwina's voice rang out. "Get in."

"Sweet! Our ride's here," Zee said, tromping through cheese to get to the door.

"With the touch of a button, I can send four thousand volts of current through the frame of this car," Edwina said. "That's twice as much as the electric chair. I suggest you back away and let Gabby get in. *Only* Gabby."

Zee held up her hands and took a giant step back. "You know what, Gabs? I'm just gonna let you get in."

"I don't know who you are," Dina shouted toward the car, "but you're getting a dry-cleaning bill for this pantsuit!"

Gabby stood. The Martian was still clinging to her jacket.

"I'll take him."

The voice belonged to a stone-faced, firm-jawed man in a dark suit and sunglasses. Gabby hadn't even seen him approach; he was just suddenly there, right next to Satchel. He bent down to take the Martian, and the doughy little alien clung to him gratefully. "Thank Fluguin you came! You have no idea what I've been through!"

As the firm-jawed man stood back to full height, Dina smiled and flipped her hair, spraying sauce in Gabby's face.

"You, sir," she said. "You seem to understand what's

happening here. Do you mind if I interview you on camera about the alien situation?"

"That would be fine," the man said with a nod. "Perhaps I could even show you my bunny collection."

Dina cocked her head, confused, but she still beckoned to her cameraman, and they followed the man across the pizza.

"Get in," Edwina said from the car. "Now, Gabby."

Gabby leaned into the car. "I will. Let me just get Sneakers and Sharli and Petey."

"They're going in another car. I assure you they're quite safe. You might have noticed we're handling this situation."

Gabby turned and looked around. Another limo was on the pizza, and Gabby saw Sneakers's tail disappear as the dog jumped in and the door slammed shut. Gabby looked out at the crowd to see how they were reacting, but most of them—including her own mother and Arlington—weren't even looking her way. Massive stage lights had appeared and snapped on around the perimeter of the picnic area, and there was now a tall platform stage with a giant screen behind it that Gabby was sure hadn't been there when she visited her mom before. The stage was far and high enough from Gabby that she couldn't see it clearly, but on the screen it was huge. A good-looking middle-aged man in a suit stood on it. He held a microphone and called down to the crowd.

"Whaddaya think, people, are you impressed? 'Cause you've all just been a part of illusionist Jack Marvel's latest special: *Mindtrip*! Let's give him a big hand!"

A dark-haired man wearing black jeans and an open black vest that showed off his insanely cut abs strolled onto the stage, arms spread wide to gather in the ecstatic cheers and applause from the crowd. He put his palms together and bowed, then took the microphone from the man in the suit.

"Thank you, everyone," he said in the low purr Gabby had seen a million times on TV. "And a big thanks to Gabby Duran, who won the online contest to be my volunteer helper. Let's give her a round of applause."

The lights moved, blinding Gabby with their glare. She put up an arm to shield her eyes. The crowd screamed and clapped, and Madison squealed, "That's my bestie! Me, Madison Murray!" but somehow under it all Gabby heard Edwina sigh and groan from the car.

"Oh, for the love of Zinqual . . ."

"And just so you know," Jack Marvel continued as the lights pivoted back to him, "the pizza did get measured before the illusion, and it was one hundred thirty-two feet across. This is officially the world's largest pizza! Give it up!"

Now the crowd really lost their minds.

"I didn't know you entered a contest to help Jack Marvel," Satchel said. "Why didn't you tell me?"

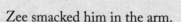

Zee smacked him in the arm.

"There are ways I can make the *car* get *you*," Edwina said, "and I assure you, you won't like them."

"Gotta go," Gabby said. She crawled halfway into the car, then stopped. She turned and looked back at her friends—Zee with her hands in her already-full overall pockets, Satchel with his shoulders slightly hunched and his hair hanging in his face. Gabby's heart swelled. They'd been her two best friends forever and she'd always loved them, but for some reason she'd never felt how much until right now.

She ran and threw her arms around Zee, then Satchel.

"I love you guys," she said. "Thanks for helping me."

Without looking back, she climbed into the limousine and slammed the door.

chapter
TWENTY-ONE

"Jack Marvel works for A.L.I.E.N.?" Gabby asked as the limousine sped away.

"Most of the big illusionists do," Edwina answered from the driver's seat without turning around. "It's a win-win partnership, really."

Gabby reached up and pulled at one of her curls. She didn't want to ask her next question, but she had to know. "So . . . you think people will believe it was all an illusion? I didn't just destroy A.L.I.E.N.?"

"Single-handedly? What a high opinion you have of yourself. No, you did not. The Jack Marvel revelation will be more than enough to debunk Ms. Parker's news story, and as for those who saw the event in person, most will be equally satisfied. A few memories will have to be altered, but nothing beyond the pale." She looked in the rearview mirror and met Gabby's eyes. "The remote control was a nice touch. People are much more open to suggestion when there's a logical explanation available. Well done."

Edwina was stingy with her praise. When Gabby received it, she normally took a moment to soak it in and enjoy, but right now she had bigger concerns. She leaned forward in her seat. "Are Petey, Sharli, and Sneakers going home?"

"They'll be gently debriefed and checked out by Medical, just like you, but yes, then they will go home. Petey's parents and Blinzarra already know the children are safe."

"Good," Gabby said. "And Blinzarra . . . now that Sharli's back—she won't push the red button, right?"

Edwina raised an eyebrow. "How do you know about the red button?"

"I'll tell you everything, just . . . will she?"

Edwina pursed her lips and turned her attention back to the road ahead. "She already has."

"What?!" Gabby cried. "But Petey said if she did, there'd be war all over the universe. He said it would hit Earth, too!"

"Petey's a bright child and a very good eavesdropper on his parents' conversations," Edwina said. "He's correct. The red button began a countdown to release the most dreadful weapon the universe has ever seen. Miravlad and Esquagon both have a stockpile. Once one is released, more will follow from both planets. Galactic allies will join in the fight. Earth will be in the crosshairs within the year, but it's only one of the planets in danger. Most likely, the entire Cosmos will devolve into UW-Six."

"UW-Six?"

"Universal War Six."

"There've been five other Universal Wars?"

Edwina sighed and shook her head. "The school systems here." Then she met Gabby's eyes in the rearview mirror again. "What do you think wiped out the dinosaurs?"

"An asteroid?"

Edwina chuckled. "Don't tell your friend the tiny Martian that. They worked very hard on that weapon. I'm sure he'd want the credit."

Gabby shook her head. She was so used to Edwina knowing everything long before Gabby did, she hadn't told her the most important thing.

"He's not my friend," Gabby said "And the Esquagonians didn't take him—or any of us. The Martians did. And the one who came back with us—the little one—he was in charge. When he was talking to the P.T.A. meeting, he wore a patch that made him *look* like an Esquagonian—"

Gabby surged forward and bumped her head as Edwina slammed on the brakes.

"Ow," Gabby said.

"Seat belt. Always." Edwina smacked both hands down on the steering wheel. "I knew it!"

"I knew it, too," Gabby said, "and I always do wear a seat belt, it's just—"

"This is not about your seat belt, Gabby!" Edwina snapped. "Though of course you should put one on. This is about Mars. They *want* UW-Six—their most profitable times are during war, and they're close enough to the Outer Reaches that they aren't affected by the fighting."

"Yeah," Gabby said, amazed that Edwina got it so quickly, "that's what I thought, too. I mean, I didn't know the history or anything, but . . . yeah."

Gabby heard horns blaring all around them. When she looked through the limousine's tinted windows, she was impressed by the sheer number of different vulgar hand signals she saw.

"Should we be stopped in the middle of the highway?" she asked.

Edwina turned all the way around in her seat. "Tell me everything. Quickly."

Gabby did. When she was done, Edwina said, "I need to make a call." She pressed one button on the dash, then another. As the partition between them rolled shut, Gabby heard her say, "Hello, Eugene?"

Then nothing else. The barrier was soundproof.

There was a tablet screen built into the front wall of the limousine, just below the partition. Gabby booted it up and clicked around to see article after article about Jack Marvel and his latest illusion. One tabloid site called out the event as a real alien sighting, but that site also had an interview with the Loch Ness Monster, so its reporting was either completely bogus or shockingly accurate. Either way, most people wouldn't believe it.

Gabby was glad she'd listened to Edwina and put her seat belt on. Even with it, she was thrown to the side as the limousine cut a sharp U-turn, inciting even more honks from the other cars on the highway.

"My superior, the chief executive overseer of A.L.I.E.N., doesn't believe your story," Edwina said as the partition came back down.

Gabby was shocked. She wasn't a liar. Did Edwina's boss think she'd lied?

"It's true! Why would I make it up? *How* would I make it up?"

Edwina didn't answer. Her lips were set in a firm line, and she held the steering wheel in a white-knuckled grip. Cars zipped by the window as the limo moved faster and faster.

"Tell your superior to ask Petey," Gabby said. "He'll say the same thing."

"I don't doubt it," Edwina said. "Petey is an imaginative child."

Gabby's jaw dropped. "You don't believe me either?! What about Sneakers? Sneakers can do that thing where he shows people what he sees. If you don't believe me, ask Sneakers!"

"It's not about me believing you," Edwina said. "It's about Eugene believing you. And while I did mention Petey and Sneakers to him as solid sources of information, he made it quite clear he has no interest in hearing from a ten-year-old boy and a dog."

Edwina sounded angry. Gabby had never heard that controlled tightness in her voice. "Eugene's your superior?"

"Yes," Edwina said, and Gabby thought she heard a sneer in the word. "He expressed doubt about the P.T.A. meeting from the beginning. He was against the treaty. He didn't believe Esquagon and Miravlad had good intentions for peace. When we heard rumblings of a threat, he suspected the Esquagonians right away. I knew it didn't add up. It took centuries of debate to get Esquagon and Miravlad to even *talk* about a treaty. It didn't make sense that their planetary governments would do anything to harm it now, and no rogue operators could pull off the operation on Earth—that's why the meeting was placed here. I said as much to Eugene, but he claimed I was being naive. When we received intelligence that Esquagonians were headed to Blinzarra's house to kidnap Sharli, he said it proved he was right."

"The text you sent me," Gabby said. "That was because you thought *Esquagonians* were coming to take Sharli?"

"That was the report, yes, but I still had my doubts, which is likely why Eugene insisted I be on the team to check it out. Four of us arrived at the house and were promptly neutralized by a team of three Esquagonians—"

"*Not* Esquagonians. Martians. With patches. And I bet they used different patches to look like me, Zee, and Satchel." Then she frowned, thinking of what Edwina had just said. "What do you mean 'neutralized'? Were you . . . ?"

"Rendered neutral," Edwina said. "By the time we were again operational, the first message from Esquagon had come through to the P.T.A. meeting. Everyone saw that an Esquagonian had kidnapped Sharli. Given that visual evidence and the evidence of my fellow agents, almost no one believed the Esquagonian ambassador's protests that Esquagon wasn't involved. Ganatel managed to keep negotiations open for as long as possible, but—"

"Ganatel's the fuzzy orange mascot woman?"

Edwina looked in the rearview mirror and shot her a withering glare. "Please tell me you did not just call the Universal Head of Cosmotic Affairs 'the fuzzy orange mascot woman.'"

Gabby shrank a little in her seat. "Wouldn't dream of it?"

Edwina nodded. "Ganatel did her best, but once Blinzarra saw the very small and disturbingly adorable Martian stack yet another accusation onto the pile against the Esquagonians, she refused to wait any longer. She pressed the red button and started the launch countdown."

"Wait, you mean what he said just now at the fair?" Gabby said. "How did she see that?"

"A.L.I.E.N. is always aware of news stories involving extraterrestrials," Edwina said. "Since this particular one involved the return of Blinzarra's daughter, of course Eugene pulled it up on the conference room screen."

"Okay," Gabby said, "but why won't he believe me? And why won't he even listen to Petey and Sneakers? We were *there*."

"There are only two reasons. Either Eugene is a

blithering idiot, or he stands to gain from a war as much as Mars," Edwina said. "And it is my experience that Eugene is *not* a blithering idiot."

Gabby took a second to let this sink in. She nodded as it all clicked in place. "You're saying Eugene is working with the Martians. They're paying him to make sure Esquagon gets blamed for Sharli's kidnapping and the war gets bigger!"

"You needn't sound so excited about it, but yes, that's what I'm saying. No doubt the Martians promised him an escape off-planet as well, so he wouldn't have to contend with the fallout on Earth."

Gabby's knee jounced up and down. She was suddenly full of energy and felt like if she didn't do anything about it she'd explode.

"So what do we do?" Gabby asked. "We have to tell somebody and stop him before the countdown ends!"

"That is the plan," Edwina said.

She hung a U-turn and slammed on the brakes, then got out of the car and opened Gabby's door. When Gabby stepped out, she saw a very familiar building with a rustic facade, designed to look like an Italian villa.

"We're going to a Pasta Garden?" Gabby asked.

The restaurant chain was everywhere. She'd eaten there a zillion times.

"We're going to the P.T.A. meeting," Edwina said.

Though her white hair and lined face proved she was a much older woman, she stood tall and moved toward the door with quick, determined strides. Gabby had to trot to catch up with her. "It's in the secret room downstairs, the one all Pasta Gardens keep reserved for any necessary A.L.I.E.N. meetings."

"The Pasta Garden works with A.L.I.E.N.?"

"Of course. How could they possibly make unlimited fresh breadsticks without cloning technology?" Edwina opened the door to the restaurant. "Let's go. We have less than five minutes until launch time."

chapter
TWENTY-TWO

The restaurant was crowded. At least twenty people hovered around the hostess podium. Edwina strode past all of them to get to the hostess herself, a girl with dark hair in a messy bun who couldn't have been more than nineteen. She looked frazzled as she tried to juggle all the voices yelling at her to find out when they'd be seated.

"Excuse me," Edwina said, "but may I see where you make your plindilini?"

The hostess was stunned, but only for a second. Then she stood tall and looked Edwina respectfully in the eye. Gabby thought she might salute. "Right this way."

She led Edwina and Gabby down a long hall, ignoring the shouts of "Hey! I thought I was next!" and "Come on, when's it my turn?" from angry customers. The hallway was covered in olive vine wallpaper, and the hostess soon stopped, looked both ways, then stood on tiptoe and placed her hand flat on a bunch of olives.

An otherwise invisible panel slid open to reveal a well-lit staircase.

"Thank you," Edwina said.

She led the way, and Gabby followed. The panel slid closed the second they crossed the threshold. All the noise from the restaurant disappeared, but Gabby didn't hear anything from the P.T.A. meeting. The stairway was clearly soundproofed—a precaution, Gabby figured, against anyone hearing something they shouldn't.

When Edwina opened the door at the bottom of the stairs, Gabby saw almost the exact scene she'd witnessed on the Martian's screen. There was the same conference table with the red button, and the same array of unique and varied aliens. This time, however, there were some differences. For starters, she hadn't noticed before that the entire table was covered with bowls of breadsticks. More importantly, no one was shouting, not even Blinzarra and the squidlike Esquagonian at the head of the table. The two of them sat back to back, arms and tentacles crossed, while the furry orange woman with the duck beak, googly eyes, and bunny ears—the Universal Head of Cosmotic Affairs who most decidedly did *not* look like a sports team mascot—crouched between them and spoke in soft, reasonable tones. Everyone else in the room was fixated on something else Gabby hadn't seen earlier: the large screen at the end of the room. Gabby was sure this was where the P.T.A. meeting had seen Sharli and Sneakers with the Martian disguised as an Esquagonian. Now it showed a countdown in large red numbers:

00:01:45 and counting.

One minute and forty-five seconds until Blinzarra launched the ultimate weapon that would plunge the Universe into war.

"I apologize for the interruption"—Edwina's voice was loud and crisp, and everyone in the room turned to face her—"but I'm here with Gabby Duran, A.L.I.E.N. Associate 4118-25125A. She was an eyewitness to the kidnapping and can confirm that it was *not* the—"

It all happened in the blink of an eye. Gabby saw a man step toward them. He was tall and bloated, with what looked like one strand of greasy gray hair wrapped around and around his head to make it seem like he wasn't bald. He pulled a wide-mouthed hair dryer from the small of his back and pointed it at her and Edwina, but in the second it took her to realize it wasn't a hair dryer, but a weapon, he had already fired twice.

The shots made no sound, but Gabby's whole body gave a single jolt like she'd received an electric shock. Next to her, Edwina jolted, too.

Then she stopped making sound as well.

Her lips continued to move for a moment, but when she realized nothing was coming out she first grabbed her throat, then glared balefully at the bloated man.

"My apologies for my employee," the man said, addressing the group. "She's acting above her pay grade and doesn't know what she's talking about. We all know who kidnapped your child, Blinzarra. And while, Ralph, I understand you *say* the order didn't officially come from Esquagon"—the man gave an exaggerated shrug and a small chuckle, just to make clear he didn't believe that for a second—"official or not, we all know who did it. Now look, I want peace as much as anybody else, but Miravlad has to have the right to defend themselves. Same as Esquagon."

Several things clicked in for Gabby as the man spoke. First, the Esquagonian ambassador was named Ralph, which was totally unexpected. Second and arguably more importantly, the bloated man had to be Eugene, Edwina's superior.

Third, Eugene was lying, which led Gabby to her fourth conclusion: their theory had been correct, and the Chief Executive Overseer of A.L.I.E.N. was secretly in cahoots with Mars, working against every other planet in the universe for his own gain.

The P.T.A. needed to know. Gabby looked at the countdown. She had exactly one minute to tell them.

"He's lying!" Gabby shouted, but the words didn't come out. Eugene's weapon had stolen her voice. Just like Edwina, she was totally mute. She tried again, waving her arms and screaming as loud as she could, but absolutely nothing came out.

Eugene turned to address someone behind Gabby. "Guards."

A hand grasped Gabby's right arm, but she kept trying desperately to talk to the P.T.A. members, even though she knew she couldn't make a sound.

Eugene, meanwhile, looked at Blinzarra, his face filled with sympathy. "I apologize for the interruption," he said, "but even more for leaving your child so vulnerable. The Unsittables program was Edwina's idea, and obviously her character judgment is lacking. Gabby Duran is clearly not qualified to watch anyone's children, never mind those of an important intergalactic diplomat such as yourself. She's a terrible babysitter."

Gabby saw red. Literally. She had never been so angry in her life.

She was a *great* babysitter. If she knew one thing in her life, she knew that. And this man—this lying, selfish, corrupt, swirly-strand-hair man—was going to tell Sharli's mom that she wasn't?

No way.

Gabby didn't care that she was in a room with the most powerful beings in the universe. She didn't care about protocol, or being polite, or following the rules. She didn't care that Eugene had stolen her voice. She was going to find a way to let this P.T.A. meeting know the truth about everything.

And she had exactly thirty seconds to do it.

The guard dragged Gabby farther back toward the door.

She couldn't tell the P.T.A. members what she'd seen, but maybe she could show them.

In a single motion, Gabby ripped her arm out of the guard's grip, swung her knapsack around, and opened the front pouch. She pulled out the pink acne-wipe patch she'd stashed there and slapped it on the back of her neck.

Gabby felt nauseous and dizzy as her head stretched long and her body mushed down. Her eyes enlarged to platters. Her legs grew and split into four, eight, sixteen, more than twenty long tentacles that writhed and undulated and squirmed.

Everyone in the room gasped. Everyone except Edwina, who simply smiled.

Gabby was an Esquagonian now, just like the Martian had been.

And in this body, she had a voice. She could feel it.

Gabby stretched out her long, sucking, popping tentacles and climbed right on top of the conference table. Her writhing limbs knocked breadstick bowls into P.T.A. members' laps, but she didn't care. She just needed to be heard.

"Blinzarra! Ralph!"

Gabby's voice grumbled and rasped. She looked at the countdown clock.

Fifteen seconds.

"Esquagon was framed by the Martians. They want the war so they can sell more weapons, and they offered Eugene a cut so he'd help," Gabby said. Out of the corner of her eye she saw Eugene try to raise his weapon again, but three different aliens jumped to their feet and held him back. "Look at me. I'm not lying. You see how they did it. Now stop that launch sequence."

Blinzarra looked stunned, like she wasn't sure she could believe her eyes.

Gabby didn't have time for that.

Eight seconds left. With everyone's eyes on her, she reached up a tentacle and ripped the pink circular patch off the back of her neck. Instantly, she was back in her own body, which felt oddly small and insubstantial. She dropped to her knees, right there on the table in front of Blinzarra . . . and right into the one remaining basket of breadsticks. Marinara dipping sauce soaked through Gabby's jeans, but they'd been through worse today.

Gabby stared into Blinzarra's eyes. Blinzarra wasn't a client now. She wasn't an important alien ambassador. She was just *wrong*, and Gabby had to make her see what was *right*.

She opened her mouth to speak, but now that she was back in her own body, her voice was gone. She kicked herself for forgetting and was about to put the patch back on when she jolted back with another electric shock.

Gabby looked over her shoulder and saw Ganatel, the fuzzy orange Universal Head of Cosmotic Affairs, had moved next to Eugene and taken his hair-dryer blaster. It was still pointed at Gabby, and Ganatel nodded at her to continue. Gabby returned the nod, then turned back to Blinzarra.

"I spent all day with your daughter today," she said, her voice back strong as ever. "Sharli's amazing. Don't be a dupe and make her live through a Universal War. Don't let

Eugene and the Martians use you and Ralph to make themselves richer. Don't do it."

Blinzarra's face hardened. She looked like she was mad at Gabby, but Gabby didn't care. As long as Blinzarra did the right thing.

And she had two seconds left to do it.

chapter
TWENTY-THREE

blinzarra tapped a spot just above her left ear.

"We've been deceived," she said. "Stop the launch sequence."

The countdown clock froze with one second left.

Everyone in the room released their collective breath.

Ganatel fixed her googly eyes on Eugene. "You and I need to talk."

"About what?" Eugene asked. He tried to look calm, but rivers of sweat poured down his puffy cheeks. "You're going to believe a child and a washed-up old agent over A.L.I.E.N.'s Chief Executive Overseer?"

"Seeing as you purposely gagged these women to keep vital information from us, yes, that's exactly what I'm going to do. The Martian who was being debriefed will remain in custody while we look into these allegations. And as for you . . ." She turned to two muscular women with purple skin. "Take him into custody."

"What?! No!" Eugene cried out as the two women took him by the elbows and led him toward the door. "This is absurd! I'm innocent! Let me go!"

"Oh, by the way, Eugene," Ganatel called out to him, "I'm the exact same age as Edwina, so please be careful how you use the words 'old' and 'washed-up.'"

Eugene turned bright red. "You . . . what? I mean . . . What I meant was . . ."

But he was already out the door. Ganatel turned to Gabby and smiled. "Thank you, Gabby. It looks like you just saved the entire universe from a terrible mistake."

Gabby felt warm all over, but it could have been the marinara sauce still seeping into her jeans. Or maybe it was the thrill of being strong enough to step up and do whatever it took to be heard.

She felt brazen. She liked it.

"You're welcome," she said. Then she plopped down cross-legged on the table, freeing the breadstick bowl from under her knee. She picked up one that wasn't overly smushed, dunked it in the remains of the marinara sauce, then took a big bite as she turned to Blinzarra and Ralph, who were having trouble meeting each other's eyes. "Soooo, Blinzarra? Ralph? Think maybe you can just *share* Blartnok 939 so the whole universe can sleep at night and not worry about a giant war destroying everything?"

Ralph looked up at the ceiling. He tented several pairs of his tentacles, popping their suction cups together and apart. Blinzarra looked down and tapped her foot on the floor. Gabby pointed the breadstick at her.

"Blinzarra . . . Sharli can share," Gabby said. "She had to learn that from you. I know you can do it, too."

Blinzarra shot Gabby an amused look. "Yes," she said. "I can share. All of Miravlad can." She held her hand out to Ralph. "Ralph, shall we agree the planet should be split equally between Miravlad and Esquagon?"

Ralph met her eyes and beamed. "Yes. Yes, we shall."

He took her hand in four of his tentacles and they shook. The room erupted in cheers, and Ganatel reached into a briefcase to pull out the actual planetary treaty that would settle their peace for good. The two leaders signed, then everyone cheered again.

"Breadsticks for everyone!" Ganatel cried. "Let the hostess know. And tell her to crank up the cloning machine—we're having never-ending pasta bowls, too!"

More cheers, and a purple-skinned man nodded and slipped out the door.

Then a loud foot-stamp echoed through the room.

It was Edwina. Her lips were pursed and her brow furrowed. She was *not* happy.

"Ah, of course," Ganatel said. "My apologies."

She picked up Eugene's hair-dryer gun and pointed it at Edwina, who reared back with the electric shock. She quickly righted herself and smoothed out her dark suit. "Certainly took you long enough," she said.

"My apologies," Ganatel said. "Would it make you feel better if I said it seems likely you have a promotion in your future? I have a feeling we'll need a new Chief Executive Overseer at A.L.I.E.N."

"You *will*," Gabby said. "Everything I said is true. Sneakers and Sharli and Petey will back me up. I can tell you the whole story."

"You can tell all of us," Ganatel said, "as we feast!"

As if on cue, the door opened and several Pasta Garden servers came in to wipe down the conference table and set up a huge array of pasta dishes and breadsticks. None of them batted an eye at the wild assortment of creatures in the room, which was pretty amazing to Gabby. She had no idea Pasta Garden jobs required such specific training and security clearance. She'd give them much more respect from now on.

As the setup went on, Gabby slid off the conference table and walked up to Edwina.

"I know the fate of the whole Unsittables program was riding on how I did today . . ." she began.

"Indeed," said Edwina. "And you succeeded in getting two of your charges kidnapped, then bringing another with you to Mars—"

"Not *that* Mars," Gabby interjected.

"Where you nearly got all four of you killed, then revealed the existence of alien life on Earth on live TV."

"True," Gabby said. "But I also saved the entire universe, sooo . . ."

The corner of Edwina's mouth curled up the littlest bit. "I'm sure it will all work out."

"Especially since you're gonna be the new head of A.L.I.E.N., right?"

Gabby chucked Edwina companionably on the arm. Edwina raised an eyebrow and looked down at her.

"We'll just stop the conversation while we're ahead," Gabby said. "Breadstick?"

The table was now fully laden with mass quantities of breadsticks and pasta, and before long everyone in the room was seated and tucking in. Gabby sat between Blinzarra and Ralph and held court, gripping everyone's attention with her vivid stories about her trip to Mars and all her other babysitting adventures. She played the room with as much virtuosity as she played her French horn, milking every laugh, gasp, and stunned silence.

Everyone was enjoying themselves so much, they barely noticed when the door opened. Then the hostess from upstairs cleared her throat. "Excuse me," she said, leaning in, "but someone told me these three were interested in plindilini?"

Gabby turned and saw Sharli was in the hostess's arms. Sneakers walked by their side, with Petey standing on his head. Gabby jumped to her feet so quickly, she knocked her chair backward.

"Petey! Sharli! Sneakers!"

She ran for the kids, but Petey's father beat her to it. He hopped onto the table, sprinted across, leaped onto Gabby's shoulder, then slid down her arm and somersaulted to a landing on Sneakers's head, where he hugged his son.

"Petey! I missed you, buddy."

"Sharli-bear!" Blinzarra cried, and Gabby held back so the woman could make her way around the table and take her daughter into her arms.

Gabby knelt down and hugged Sneakers, being careful not to jostle Petey and his dad.

"You're a good dog, Sneakers," she told him. "The best."

When their parents had finished hugging them tight, Gabby hugged Sharli and gave Petey a high five. "You three are the most amazing kids I've ever babysat," she declared. "And I sit for a lot of kids."

"Didja tell them?" Petey asked. "Didja tell 'em the best part?"

"That you took the acne-wipe patch and turned yourself into an Esquagonian?"

"No."

"That you programmed the transport pod to get us back to Earth?"

"Nah. That's cool, but come on!"

"That you dove through lasers so we could get to Sharli and Sneakers?"

"No! That Blinzarra used the *S*-word! And I heard it!"

Petey danced on the conference table while his dad looked on, amused. Blinzarra blushed.

"You must all be hungry after your adventure," Blinzarra said, changing the subject. "Want breadsticks and pasta?"

"Yeah!" cried Petey, and Sharli echoed him with a "YAH!" Sneakers barked.

Everyone went back to the table and listened to the whole story again, but from Petey's perspective, with Gabby throwing in commentary and reenacting the best bits with him. She was so involved in the storytelling, she didn't even notice when Edwina and Ganatel pushed back from the table and retreated to a far corner to speak privately.

"Your protégée did well," Ganatel said.

"She saved the universe," Edwina replied.

"We still have to do it, though. Her story is what's going to bring down the Martian Empire. She'll have enemies."

Edwina nodded. "I know."

"I wouldn't if there were a better way," Ganatel said. "We'll all be forever grateful to her, but it's for her own good."

"There's just so much to alter," Edwina said. "She'll change."

Ganatel shrugged. "Sometimes change is good."

Edwina thought about that as she watched Gabby capture the attention of the entire room, jumping up to act out the most dramatic moments of her adventures in front of the most powerful creatures in the universe. There was a time when she would have shied away from that; now she was in her element. "You're right," she said. "Sometimes change is good."

"Of course, it won't be just her. Her mother and sister will certainly need attention, and probably her two best friends. Everyone else will accept the easy explanation: mother got a job out of town, family had to leave right away. We've both seen it work a million times."

"Indeed," Edwina said, "and I believe I know the perfect new location."

"Do you have a location in mind?" Ganatel asked.

"Havensburg."

Ganatel raised a fuzzy orange eyebrow. "Havensburg? That's a hub."

"I know," Edwina said. "It'll be good to have her available. Just in case."

"Even though she'll be different? Even though she won't remember any of this?"

"She won't need to," Edwina said. "She'll be different, but at heart she'll be the same. And when the time comes, she'll be ready."

"I believe you're right," Ganatel said. Then she sighed. "I suppose it's time."

"Yes," Edwina agreed. "But don't use the bunny. She knows that one."

"Understood."

Ganatel walked out of the room, only to return a few moments later with something cradled in her arms.

"Everyone, you won't believe what one of the waiters found outside. A stray kitten!"

Every creature in the room got to its feet to see it. The tiny gray tabby sat cuddled in Ganatel's fuzzy arms. It mewed adorably and everyone said "Awwww" in such complete unison that they had to laugh.

"Can I hold it?" said an otter-man with horns.

"Aw, I'd like to hold it." This from a globule with feet.

"I wanna hold it!" said Petey, and when his dad raised an eyebrow, he added, "What? I'm strong. I helped save the universe!"

"Gabby should hold it first," Ralph said. "She helped save the universe, too."

"Aw. Thanks, Ralph," Gabby said.

Ganatel walked to her, and Gabby melted as she took the kitten into her hands. It was small enough to fit into her palm and looked up at her with big, blue, mesmerizing eyes. If it were really a stray, maybe Alice would let her and Carmen keep it.

"It's so sweet," Gabby said.

"Go ahead, Gabby," Ganatel said gently. "Pet the kitten."

Gabby did, and Edwina looked on. The old woman took a deep breath and swallowed a lump in her throat.

"Until we meet again, Gabby Duran," she said. "Until we meet again."

Acknowledgments

First, thank you a million times over to everyone who has read and enjoyed Gabby's dossiers. We appreciate you, we love hearing from you, and we're so honored you've embraced Gabby and her adventures. Thanks for joining us on this fourth outing; the series wouldn't exist without you.

Kieran Viola, there truly aren't enough words for us to properly sing your praises. We love working with you, we love your passion for Gabby, and we love your notes. You are an editor par excellence, and we're lucky to have you. We're also eager to plug you, so, readers, please enjoy Kieran's author side at www.kieranscott.net.

Huge thanks also to everyone else at Hyperion who helped us on this book: Emily Meehan, Mary Mudd, and Vanessa Moody in editorial; Marci Senders for her cover art; Sara Liebling and Guy Cunningham in managing editorial/copyediting; Elke Villa and Seale Ballenger in marketing/publicity.

In addition, we're incredibly excited that *Gabby Duran and the Unsittables* will soon be airing on Disney Channel, and we're monumentally thankful for everyone who helped make that happen. The list is long, but we'd especially like to give a grateful shout-out to Nancy Kanter for believing in the project. We cannot thank you enough, nor can we imagine putting Gabby into better hands. Kudos also to Mike Alber and Gabe Snyder for so expertly making the leap from Gabby's book world to her television world, and thanks to the entire team of people involved with the show—we've loved what we've seen and can't wait for the rest of the world to see it too. Special thanks to Pat Van Note and Miriam Ogawa, who were instrumental in helping us bridge those two worlds—it was a true pleasure.

Jane Startz, as always, we owe you everything. You brought us together and started it all. We are so grateful to have you in our lives. Thanks also to Mayde Alpi for all your help along the way. To Matthew Saver, our attorney, thank you for all your gracious wisdom and work on our behalf.

On a personal note, Elise wants to thank her husband Randy, daughter Maddie, and dog Jack-Jack. Everything good in my life starts with you. I raise a glass to those I miss terribly: Mom-Mom Eva, Pop-Pop Irv, and Pop-Pop Nate; and I raise a glass even higher to Mom-Mom Sylvia, who just turned ONE HUNDRED AND THREE. I am beyond lucky to have you in my life, and can't wait until I see you again.

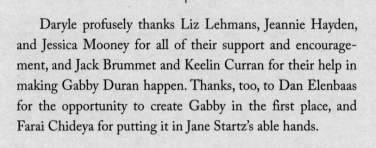

Daryle profusely thanks Liz Lehmans, Jeannie Hayden, and Jessica Mooney for all of their support and encouragement, and Jack Brummet and Keelin Curran for their help in making Gabby Duran happen. Thanks, too, to Dan Elenbaas for the opportunity to create Gabby in the first place, and Farai Chideya for putting it in Jane Startz's able hands.